Lawman's Justice

A Sheriff Clay Holland Adventure
2 Novels

Lawman's Justice

A Sheriff Clay Holland Adventure
2 Novels

By

William S. Hubbartt

Table of Contents

Chapter 1

"...he may be out there, but he ain't lost..."

The snow had been falling for two days now, accumulating to twelve inches with drifts reaching knee-high, and higher in some areas as the wicked winds blew off the Edwards Plateau down across the open west Texas plains. The structures in Bent Creek covered in white powder gave an appearance more of lonely gravestones on boot hill rather than a living thriving community. Folks hid in their tiny homes and shanties huddled around fireplaces and potbellied stoves. Only a few stalwarts ventured forth, and only when absolutely necessary for essentials such as firewood, water, or feed for the animals.

Winter had hit early, and hard, with temperatures plunging well below the usual low-forties customary for a Texas December. It had begun with a heavy rain, which turned to snow as temperatures plummeted and the snow piled up. Now, the below-freezing temps were made harsher by relentless winds, blowing the icy powder through cracks and crevices of doors and windows and corners where the weathered wood had separated.

Sheriff Clay Holland was one of the stalwart few, tromping his solid six-two stature through the knee-high drifts between buildings, making his way towards the Cattleman's Saloon, the premier watering hole for the cowboys and settlers of Bent Creek. He told himself he needed to make his daily rounds to check the town, knowing in reality that he would warm up with a few shots of Sam's best whiskey. He shivered in the cold and pulled the wool-lined drover coat tighter around his neck while hanging on to his Stetson with his free hand. In his fifty-five years, he could recall only one winter as fierce, in the early 1860s, the one the old-timers referred to it as little ice age.

The virgin snow showed no tracks that others had ventured forth. With the horizontal blowing snow, it was hard to see from one building to the next. The snow blew up over the planked walkway in front of the saloon, making it impossible to find the step, causing him to stumble over a frozen watering trough up onto the walkway.

"Ow, oh shit," blurted Clay as he landed on all fours and twisted to catch his hat before it blew away. "Sam! You in there?"

"That you, Clay?"

"Open the damn door!"

There was a creak, then a clunk as the door was wrenched free. The Sheriff stumbled in along with a gust of wind and blowing snow. Sam quickly leaned against the door to slam it closed and to secure it from blowing loose by the wind. Bits of the white powder skittered through the air from the cracks in between the door and its frame.

"I'm getting too old for this," said the Sheriff as he limped in, an old injury re-aggravated by the fall. He unwrapped a scarf and pulled the long drover coat from his shoulders. "I need a stiff one, maybe two. It may take a few minutes to warm up today."

A bottle clinked onto the bar and gurgled as Sam poured a glass for his best customer. The Sheriff swallowed first and blew an exhale as the fiery liquid burned his throat. Then scanned the room seeing only the resident card shark Leverett Brockton III cards spread on the table in an angular solitaire fashion next to a glass and companion bottle of whiskey.

"Mornin' Sheriff, nice to see you about this fine day. Care for some two-handed solitaire or perhaps war?" The tired-looking gambler struck a match on the table and lit the stub of a cigar, creating a cloud of smoke over the cards. His white linen suit was well worn, wrinkled, and whiskey stained, having lost the luster of days gone by when the gambler worked the riverboats on the Mississippi. "Always happy to offer a law enforcement discount to the ante."

"I'll keep my shirt, thank you," said the Sheriff. His eyes remained on the gambler but he spoke over his shoulder to bartender Sam, "You hear from Smith? Did he make it back from Kansas?"

"Shoulda been back by now, it's been over two months. But no one from Smith's place has come into town. Now, with the snow,…" Sam didn't want to put his concerns into words.

"I heard tell he was going try the railhead at Ellsworth," added the Sheriff.

The windows rattled as a gust of wind blew whistled outside, blowing a dusting of snow crystals through the crack of the front door. The men inside turned in unison to watch as the snowflakes drifted in and dropped to the floor.

"I've got a twenty dolla' gold piece says he didn't make it in before the storm," chimed in the gambler.

"Oh hell, Brockton, you son of a bitch. You'll put a bet on anything!" Sam flared. "Our town's most prominent citizen could be out there, in that blizzard, turned around or going in circles."

"Well, I'll tell you this," said the Sheriff as he lit a cigarette. "My old partner knows his way around Texas, blizzard or no, just by the slope of the ground and the direction of the streams. We spent enough time Rangering in the open country chasing Comanches and Bandidos that we can find our way day or night, in snow or rain or dust storm. I can tell you this, he may be out there, but he ain't lost."

Just then, there was the sound of a horse whinny and the clump of boots on the wooden walkway in front of the saloon. The door shook and burst open with a cloud of snow along with two bundled cowhands, coated in white powder looking like a pair of polar bears. A lantern over the bar flickered from the force of the wind as the door was slammed shut with the same force as the entry by the snow-covered pair. The room's occupants stood in silent amazement as the two snowmen lumbered heavily towards the bar.

"Well, if it ain't that son of a bitch Clay Holland! I hear-tell you was in these parts!" The first snowman shook the white powder from his drover coat, untied his black Stetson began slapping the snow away and pulled a scarf from around his neck, and dropped buffalo skin mitts onto the table. He turned and a swift punch hit the right arm of the Sheriff.

"Bonner? Is that you?" What brings you to my town?" The Sheriff recognized an old friend he hadn't seen in some time.

"I found him lost and stumbling along the San Antone trail just out of town." Now unwrapped as well, former Ranger and prominent rancher James Smith gave a back-slap to his fellow snow-man Texas Ranger Bonner O'Toole.

"Sam, some whiskeys for my friends!" said the Sheriff. He turned to the gambler who remained seated at the table with cards spread about in a new solitaire game. "Brockton, ya owe me that twenty-dollar gold piece. Smith here ain't lost; in fact, he out rounding up strays in this blizzard."

After some laughs and a few rounds of whiskey, rancher Smith described some highlights of the trail drive. Yes, they had gone to Ellsworth, prices were fair for a late-season drive, but he wouldn't give specifics, and that the animals were shipped east on the Kansas Pacific Railroad. After a couple of days in town, they headed back, running into the storm on the last two days out. Smith had come to town despite the storm in need of some critical supplies and had run into Bonner O'Toole near the road to San Antonio.

"I remember you as a young recruit, still wet behind the ears," said the Sheriff. "We were on the trail of Quanah Parker out towards Llano Estacado. That gutsy Indian threw some tough charges in our direction, but I remember that you held up your end of the line when we beat them back."

"Then you retired, missing out on all that fun," said Bonner. "But I see that you're still in the game wearing a badge. How long you been here? Say, how's that little woman of yours? What's her name?"

Clay Holland blanched with that last question. James Smith cut in and responded to the question. "Stage robbery over San Antone way, don't you remember Bonner…"

"Four years now. Uh, Sarah, she died five and a half years ago. Stage robbery like James said. But I caught up to him last summer. Sumbitch left a trail of bodies and stolen horses and kept shooting at me, so I gave him a little six-bullet justice." The Sheriff's voice had an edge, emotion tinged with anger as the memories came flooding back.

"Hey, I'm sorry man, yeh, I did hear that, and I heard you caught that guy. Sarah was a fine lady." Bonner tried to right his wrong.

"So, Ranger O'Toole, what brings you to Bent Creek?" repeated Sheriff Holland.

"Captain wants me to find the ghost bandit. Mexican fella they call *Bandido Fantasma*."

4

Chapter 2

...fists flying, arms and legs flailing...

Cold weather, some wind, and a foot of snow did not stop the sturdy Texans from important errands. The snow was still thick on the ground, but gradually a few paths had been stomped down by adventurous souls or those in a dire emergency who needed to come to town or to the store or the saloon. Sheriff Holland had two prisoners in his jail and needed to make daily rounds to the Red-eye where proprietor Betsy Brown would prepare two meals a day for the prisoners. Before the heavy snow hit, Betsy would bring the fixings to the Sheriff's office and jail. But negotiating deep snow was very difficult in a long dress and petticoats, and since the blizzard, Sheriff Holland had been walking down to the Red-eye to pick up the meals.

The heart of Bent Creek was basically two blocks long, with a scattering of homes spread out from the main street. So, a daily walk through the snow from one end to the other was just a good stretch of the legs. After a while, pathways were beaten down, though slippery. Of course, the Sheriff always stopped at the Cattleman's Saloon on his way to and from the Red-eye.

One day, as the Sheriff came out of the Cattleman's he heard loud angry voices, an argument, coming from McCann's Mercantile. A wagon with two horses stood outside the store, the animals restless and stomping in response to the intensity of emotion that emanated from inside the store. The Sheriff recognized the rig as belonging to sheepherder Donald MacDonald. He

5

followed in others' footprints through the deep snow to cross the street to the store.

"You said they would be here by now! I'm still waiting!" MacDonald was a tall man accustomed to intimidating others with his size and aggressiveness. His voice carried across the street.

"Calm down Mac Donald, there's no need to yell. It won't make them come any faster." McCann had operated his store in Bent Creek for five years now and had learned to deal with the quirks and desires of his customers. While this was the only store around for thirty miles, he tried to be responsive rather than assuming a "take it or leave it" posture.

"Where I come from, a man's word is his bond. I can't take you at your word."

"But I never promised delivery, I merely relayed the anticipated shipping date from the merchant distributer in San Antonio. Your shears will be here when they get here, like everything else."

"You think you're such a big shot,---" There was a crash of glass as a bucket hit the window and crashed through the window at the front of the store.

"Why you…"

They tangled and two bodies came tumbling out the door of the store just as the Sheriff reached the wagon, its team of horses lurching to get clear of the fighting men. The Sheriff had to jump out of the way of the scared horses. The two men were rolling about on the plank walkway in front of the store, fists flying, arms and legs flailing as each struggled to get the best of the other. The Sheriff considered letting the wrestling match continue until they tired, or one prevailed. It was clear that neither was adept in grappling or use of fists. He decided to step in.

"Stop this. MacDonald! McCann, Stop this." The grapplers were oblivious, so the Sheriff picked up the bucket and clanged it against the porch pillar in front of the store next to the fighting men. It still had no effect. The men were still intent on pounding sense into each other. Finally, the Sheriff grabbed MacDonald's arm, pulling him up from the storekeeper, and sent a right cross-connecting on the sheep herder's chin sending him out into the snow-covered street, into a wet spot where his team had been standing and urinated while they waited. Behind him, on the plank boards, sat merchant McCann, his face and mouth bloodied, wheezing gasps of air.

"What, the...I'm all wet, this,...you threw me into a puddle of horse piss," blabbered MacDonald slipping and falling again as he tried to get up. He stumbled to his feet, arms and legs churning to reach the Sheriff, who cocked another right causing the bumbling sheepherder to finally stop. MacDonald wobbled exhausted, and then bent over hands on his knees, sucking air into his tired lungs.

"What the hell was this about?" demanded the Sheriff.

"He's holding out on me!" accused MacDonald.

"Holding out what?" The Sheriff stood between the men so that they would not start up this senseless brawl. "What are you so all-fired pissed off about?"

"My shears. I ordered shears, he said they'd be in by now." MacDonald had caught his breath and still had a bit of fight in him, edging closer towards the storekeeper who remained slumped against the front of his store.

"They're coming, I didn't promith a date," mumbled the storekeeper through a bloodied mouth now missing a tooth.

"Shears? This is about shears?" Now the Sheriff was angry, letting it erupt over the stupidity of the issue that had led to fisticuffs. "Look around you. You're in a foot of snow, there's no deliveries, no stage, no nothing. And furthermore, even I know that you don't shear no sheep in the middle of winter, they'll freeze to death."

MacDonald stood there, mouth agape, finally silenced.

"You better make arrangements to pay for the repair to the store window, or you're going to spend a night in my jail for disturbing the peace," said the Sheriff. He turned and hi-stepped across the street toward the Red-eye for one of Betsy's fine steaks and a whiskey.

Chapter 3

"What's the story about this ghost feller?"

It had been a month since the December blizzard that had buried Bent Creek and the surrounding west Texas area. Temperatures had returned to normal ranges hovering near forty degrees at night and reaching close to fifties by mid-day. The snow had melted, leaving a muddy mess for nearly a week before the ground finally began to dry out. Stagecoach service had been suspended during the blizzard and afterward until the roads cleared.

Texas Ranger Bonner O'Toole took advantage of the lull in travel activity by sticking close at hand at the Cattleman's Saloon for drinks and a daily visit to The Red-eye Saloon. The sizzle of a freshly seared steak grabbed the senses only seconds before the savoring aroma filled the room. A Texas man's gotta have his seared beef with fresh bread and whatever vegetables can be had on the plains.

This was the regular routine of Sheriff Holland, and the two lawmen spent the time getting caught up on old news from the Rangers and as well as enjoying the company of Red-eye proprietor Betsy Brown and partaking of her fine cooking. Betsy was a fine-looking woman with a couple of attractive kitchen girls helping out, so the men tended to end up there for good food and pleasant company after a day of drinking with the boys at the Cattleman's.

They were able to make the rounds to the businesses in town, talking to Doc, Harold McCann, owner of the general store in town, and Washington at the stable. With each passing day after the blizzard, additional townspeople from Bent Creek and the surrounding area ventured forth and came to town.

"So, what's the story about this ghost feller? What did you call him?" asked the Sheriff as they sipped whiskeys at the Cattleman's. Gambler Leverett Brockton III had a game going with two of the area cowboys who had some time on their hands.

"He's called *Bandido Fantasma*, meaning ghost bandit in Spanish." Bonner lit a cigarillo creating a cloud of smoke. "The Captain sent me over this way because of some reported incidents, trail suggesting he's headed this way. You ain't heard of him?"

"Well, I do recall one or two reports of petty theft. Jonesie was complaining that some kids showed up one day and the next day he noticed that some tools were missing. Then out east, Herb Conover reported that a couple of head o' cattle were missing, something he noticed after seeing a lone wagon heading towards town. Animals walk away all the time, ya just round them up. But it's hardly what I'd call rustling, nothing like the days when that Mexican feller, Manuel Chavez was terrorizing the ranches north of the river."

"But them kids, are they from one of the nearby ranching families just feeling their oats, or are they strangers?" His eyes darted over to the cowboys in the card game. The Sheriff nodded in acknowledgment of the gesture.

"Hey, Deever! You're one of Jonesie's hands right?" The Sheriff called over to the card table.

"Umm, hmm." Deever was concentrating on his hand, trying to figure out whether to stand or draw some cards.

"Two bits to you if you're staying in, couple of hot ones in the deck if you want to draw," encouraged gambler Brockton.

"Deever, you'd do better to fold on this hand. You'll thank me later." The Sheriff could see over Deever's shoulder at the pair of treys and knew that Gambler Brockton always held a better hand than what he dealt. "Jonesie said some kids came by last week, then some tools were missing. You see them kids, Deever? Know if they were local, or strangers?"

"Uh, crap." Deever threw the hand down his hand and stood and turned around to talk to the Sheriff and the Ranger. "Uh, no. I seen 'em, didn't know any of 'em. Dark hair 'n' skin, look to be Mexican, maybe Indian, you know?"

"They been by before? Any of them talk to you," queried Bonner. The cowboy shook his head and reached into his pocket for some chaw.

"How many? Boys? Girls? Ages?"   Bonner queried. He had that unassuming smile underneath a thick mustache that charmed people into talking. "I mean, kids out alone in this big wide country? Think about it, were they walking, or riding an animal or in a wagon?"

"Ya know," said Deever as he worked the chaw under his lip, "two of 'em boys, talked low and fast, like them Mexican's talk. I don't know them words. When I came back they were gone and then later Jonsie says he's missing them tools he uses for turning and working the garden. And a calf, can't find the calf. The cow's fit to be tied."

"Maybe we should take a ride out there tomorrow, have a look around," said the Sheriff.

There was noise outside, hooves pounding and the rattle of the stagecoach as it rolled into town for a brief stop and change of teams. Deever went back to his game and Bonner poured another whiskey while the Sheriff walked across the street to check on any news from San Antonio.

"How's the roads," the Sheriff asked the driver, as a stranger climbed down, hair slicked back and dressed all spiffy-like, kinda like a St. Louis Gambler. Nose in the air, the stranger looked up and down the two-block long street through Bent Creek, then he hoisted a carpetbag suitcase over his shoulder and walked over towards the Red-eye.

"Getting better, still sloppy in the low spots, though. I left the mail with Mac, in the store. I hear that the circuit judge is back on schedule, gonna out this way soon. What's Miss Betsy got cooking today?"

The Sheriff answered by rubbing his stomach and giving a big smile. "Tell Miss Betsy I'll be by for dinner in a bit."

Chapter 4

"Some say he be the ghost of Chavez."

"Morning Washington, This here's my friend Bonner O'Toole, Texas Ranger," Sheriff Holland made an introduction as the two lawmen walked into the stable.

"Yessa, morning, suh, We met the other day. Morning Ranger 'Toole. Your animal she ready to go." The hostler of the Bent Creek Stable was a former Buffalo Soldier, a man who knew horses and how to care for them. "You be taking the roan today, Sheriff? I'll have her ready in a jiffy."

Washington offered an apple treat for both animals as the riders mounted and headed out of town on the southbound trail towards the Jones Ranch. The morning was crisp, with a light breeze. Most of the snow had melted except for a few drifts on north ridges hidden from the sun. Overhead a mix of clouds and spots of blue sky, gave a hint of clearing. A hawk circled overhead riding the breeze, watching for unwary prey below. The Sheriff's eyes caught a glimpse of movement to the side, and he watched as a black-tailed jackrabbit froze, its tan color blending with the surrounding dried bunchgrass. The animal's ears turned to track the two riders. Overhead, the hawk glided southward with the wind.

A half an hour later they rode up to the Jones Ranch. A modest split wood ranch house dominated by a river-rock stone fireplace sat on a small dome hill surveying the surrounding land with a barn, corral, and a couple of small outbuildings. Bonner gestured toward the noise coming from the barn, clanging metal, like the work of a blacksmith or farrier. The lawmen tied their horses in front and called out to announce their presence.

"Hello, Jones! Hey Jonesie,…Clay Holland here!"

The clanging sound stopped, "Hey! Back here, come around to the back."

The Sheriff and the Ranger walked around the barn and found a small three-sided shelter with a small forge and blower, its fire raging, and a sweaty man in a long apron with tools in hand shaping a horseshoe. On the walls hung a variety of hand forging tools used by blacksmiths and farriers. Jones gestured to the visitors to wait a minute as he gave a couple more clanging swings to the piece on the anvil, held it up with a tong, looked at both sides, checked a measure to another piece, and nodded in approval. He dunked the piece in water causing it to sizzle and steam, and then set the piece aside along with the tools.

"Hey Sheriff, what brings you out this way?"

"Jonsie, this here's my friend, Texas Ranger Bonner O'Toole, we worked together back in the day. He still carries the Ranger Star."

Bonner and Jonesie nodded in acknowledgment of each other, no other words were necessary at the moment. The Sheriff took the lead. "The Rangers received a report about a feller called the ghost bandit. This ain't a feller I've had any complaints about, so we're checking around. You run across this feller?"

"Hmm, ghost bandit? I ain't heard of nobody like that," replied Jonsie, then he smiled like there was some joke that the Sheriff might be playing. "Yer not pullin' my leg are ya? A ghost bandit? This guy dead or what?"

"Naw, they call him the ghost bandit because nobody's seen 'im," replied Bonner.

Jonsie still had a smirk on his face, thinking that the Sheriff was joshing him. "So he says Boo and scares you into giving away yer money or yer stock? How do you know the ghost is a he?"

"Ya got a point there," said Bonner. "We was talking to your man,…what's his name?" The question was directed to Sheriff Holland.

"Deever. Your man Deever said that some kids came by the other day and now you're missing some tools. What can you tell us about that?" asked the Sheriff.

"Deever seen them, I didn't. but I'm missing an ax, spade, knife, a rope, and now we can't find the baby calf."

Bonner was walking around the work shed looking at tools and down on the ground checking for a sign, or any evidence of visitors. "Any trail signs? Where'd the cow and the calf hang out?"

Jonesie was vague on details, said the cow stuck with the herd and the cattle roamed the fields for the best grasses. He hadn't seen anybody, just knew some things were gone. The Sheriff and Bonner circled around the property finding that the trails showed tracks of various animals, and horses, but could not find any clear evidence of children present. They headed off towards Herb Conover's ranch east of Bent Creek off the road to San Antonio. Herb said nothing appeared to be missing and he said he "hadn't seen any kids or anyone looking like no ghost bandit."

The better part of a day was gone with no real leads. They headed back to town. "I wonder if maybe this feller Deever's been hitting the sauce a bit too hard," said Bonner. "Maybe his imagination is running away. He been known for stories?"

"No more than the rest of us," replied the Sheriff as he rode into Bent Creek. As they walked the horses into the stable, the Sheriff struck up a conversation with hostler Washington. As the old negro led the animals to their respective stalls, he chewed on a small gob of spruce tree resin, a treat he learned about from the Indians, working it around in his mouth. In his younger years, he had been a Buffalo Soldier, part of the 10th Cavalry unit based in Kansas.

"Washington, you keep a good ear to the ground. Have you seen or heard anything about feller referred to as the ghost bandit?" asked the Sheriff.

Washington smiled at the question. That seemed to be the typical reaction to questions about this ghost bandit. "Yessa, Sheriff. I heard of the one they call *Bandido Fantasma*. That mean ghost bandit." He paused and glanced around the stable as if checking to see if anyone else was present. " But, I have not seen this *Bandido Fantasma*."

"What do you know? What do they say?"

"He seem to appear after you and Mista Smith kill the outlaw Manuel Chavez and catch the stolen herd. Some say that he be the ghost of Chavez." Washington worked the chewy spruce resin in his mouth, and spit sideways to the ground. "Me, I not see this ghost. No suh."

"You said 'some say,' who's talking about this ghost feller? Who saw him?"

"Uhm, some be travelers, passing through, I not know names. The stage driver from San Antonio, he speak of it one time, maybe a month or two ago."

"So, do you believe....?" The Sheriff left the question unfinished.

Washington smiled big, showing white teeth against coffee dark skin, enjoying the mystery. "Nobody has story that he really seen this *Bandido Fantasma*. Is it the spirit of outlaw Chavez? Or is it somebody else stepping in to replace the bandit?" Washington shrugged his shoulders and his hands rose open, "He is called *Bandido Fantasma*. I believe he is a Mexican."

Chapter 5

"I hereby call this court in session."

The day had finally come, and the people of Bent Creek were abuzz, word had preceded the arrival of the stage. Circuit Judge Hiram Jackson would be arriving in town today to conduct the murder trial for Bobby Carroll, the man who had admitted his role in the lynching last fall of Abraham Lincoln Washington, a sixteen-year-old negro youth, son of hostler Washington. The trial also would consider the shooting of Sheriff Clay Holland by upstart Johnny Barton, a gun-hand and former ranch hand for the Smith Ranch. The trials had been delayed because Judge Jackson had experienced a flare-up of his gout condition.

The judge's regular schedule called for a visit to Bent Creek about every three months, but, the most recent visit had been delayed for another month because the judge was bed-ridden for a period while the doctor in San Antonio tried various remedies to reduce the swelling and pain in his legs that had spread to his back, making him totally disabled. The judge had switched to riding a carriage instead of making his rounds on horseback, but the most recent flare-up had been really debilitating, preventing the planned late fall court appearance. The prisoners were held in the Bent Creek jail for the period.

There was a knock on the door of the Sheriff's office and jail, and the door swung open immediately. Washington came in quickly, breathing heavily in excitement. The deputy badge was pinned to his shirt. He had assisted in escorting prisoners to and from court during the last session.

"Good morning Sheriff. Judge Jackson is at the Cattleman's Saloon, and folks is gathering around, eager for court to start. Mr. Sam, he know what to do now, got it all ready for the judge and Miss Amanda, she have a special table set by the door for the womenfolk who can come in the Cattleman's for the trial. I can do deputy work if you need me."

"Thank you, Washington. I'll check with the Judge on which case he plans to hear first, and then let you know."

The Cattleman's Saloon was already filling up as Bent Creek townspeople and area ranchers gathered to observe the proceedings. The saloon had the biggest room in town that would accommodate a large number of people in one space. Women were permitted entry to the saloon only during the court sessions and all serving of drinks was suspended during court. Several small children scampered about, a yapping dog close at their heels. A young mother scurried after them and pulled them by their arms to a chair in the back.

"Good morning Judge, you're looking fit," said the Sheriff, even though the man looked a bit thinner and less robust than his last visit, his clothes hanging loosely on a thinner frame. There was no drink at the table now designated as the judge's bench, so the Sheriff signaled to proprietor Sam to bring a whiskey for the Judge and himself.

"Well, looking and feeling are two different things. It feels good to be up and around, but there's still some aches and pains, that gout got quite a hold on my joints, couldn't get out of bed for near a month. Sorry to delay these important. proceedings." The Judge smiled as whiskey found its way to his hand, and he took a big swallow. "Ahh, cure for a parched throat."

The Sheriff gulped a matching swallow, and exhaled the fiery vapors, "Damn right! So which case shall we start with? Murder, or attempted murder?"

"The murder charge is the lynching of the negro boy, right?" asked the Judge, and the Sheriff nodded affirmatively. "There might be a hanging on that one, so let's start with the attempted charge, that smart-aleck who thought he could out-draw you."

The Sheriff finger-summoned a young man and whispered to his ear, and the boy ran from the saloon turned courthouse to deliver a message to the

Deputy. Then, at the Judge's gesture, the Sheriff signaled Sam to stop serving drinks. Judge Jackson said, "young man. Call this court to order."

The Sheriff slammed his empty glass down hard on the tabletop, getting everyone's attention. Heads turned to the front of the saloon, and talking stopped. "Listen up! I hereby call this court into session. The circuit court of Bent Creek County, Texas is hereby in session. Judge Hiram Jackson presiding. The sale of likker is hereby suspended until we break for lunch."

It took a few minutes for the room to quiet; several glasses clinked as the liquor remark prompted another sip. By then, Washington led in the prisoner Johnny Barton, his hands tied behind his back. Looking unshaved and disheveled with long unkempt hair, the young gunslinger stared defiantly at the Sheriff, and then the Judge before turning his angry glare towards the Bent Creek townspeople in the court gallery at the back of the saloon. One of the women at the back row of chairs gasped nervously; a few heads turned in her direction, causing her to blush.

The Judge, a man of small stature but strong presence, banged his gavel. "Sheriff, you may begin, what are the charges against this man?"

"He's charged with attempted murder. Without cause or provocation, he drew his gun and fired on me." The sheriff glared hard at the young man now seated in a witness chair next to the Judge, a rope around his hands and an ankle chain circled the brass foot rail in front of the bar.

"And yet, here you stand today," observed the Judge with an unseen wink to the Sheriff. There were several chuckles from the room. "Now, I need a jury. You six there, standing at the bar. For this case, you are my jury. Sheriff, any of them witnesses to this matter?"

The Sheriff gave a negative shake of his head. The Judge continued his instruction. "You fellers pay attention. And when we're done, I'm gonna ask if you think he's guilty. Sheriff, call your first witness."

"The government calls Leverett Brockton III to the stand." As the sole law enforcement official in this town on the Texas plains, the sheriff served a dual role of law enforcer and prosecutor in court proceedings.

Ever the showman, gambler Leverett Brockton III stood, straightened his worn faded white linen coat, and marched chin-up to the witness chair on the other side of the Judge's table. Enjoying his moment as the center of attention, he nodded at several in the gallery who watched. The Judge held out a well-worn Bible and asked, "Do you swear to tell the truth?"

"I do indeed kind sir."

"Mr. Brockton, were you present in this establishment last fall when the defendant, Johnny Barton entered that doorway there, and drew and fired his gun, hitting me, here, under the rib, in an attempt to kill me?" The sheriff raised his shirt from under his belt and revealed a jagged rounded scar of a bullet wound on the left side of his stomach. There was a hushed mummer from those watching, heads straining to see the scar.

"Yes sir, I was."

"Please tell the court what happened."

"Well, we were playing a game of cards, and you came in asking if anybody knew about the lynching of that …. that young negro boy. And then Johnny shows up at the door, and he's lookin' for a fight, and he draws, and…and he shoots you there, like you showed."

"And then what happened?"

"Well you were hurt and had to sit, and Johnny, he ran out the door and made a break for it, but you got a piece of him, because there was a blood trail, and uh, yer deputy was able to bring him in."

The Sheriff continued questioning the other witnesses who were present, all giving similar stories that Johnny Barton had come in and drew and fired first, shooting the town's sheriff, and had then escaped.

"Do you have anything to say for yourself, young man?" asked the Judge.

"Wull, he accused me of lynching that blackie. He called me a liar. Them's fighting words. Ya just don't let people get away with that."

"Is it your assertion, Mr. uh,…Barton, that the Sheriff here called you a liar, in the course of his investigation of a death, and that justified your shooting him?" asked the Judge.

"Yeh, don't nobody call me a liar!" Johnny Barton growled.

"Sheriff, your response," directed the Judge.

"Well, as I recall, Johnny came in saying that the boy deserved a lynching, and I asked if that meant that he, Barton, here, did in fact lynch the young man. As I asked some more questions, Barton here said I called him a liar and he drew and shot me."

"Does anyone else have other facts pertinent to this matter?" the Judge asked the gallery seated in the crowded room. All were silent, a few heads turning to see if others had any remarks. The Judged turned around to the men at the bar who had been designated as a jury. "Jurors, do you have a verdict?

Does the Sheriff's questions to a man about the commission of a crime constitute grounds for shooting a law officer performing his duties? If not, you must find this man guilty of attempted murder."

The men at the bar looked at each other, and a couple shook their heads. Then one man at the far end of the bar spoke up. "Well, your honor, iffen the Sheriff was just asking a question and not makin' a statement, it ain't no lie. So, it seems that Johnny here was just itchen for a fight and he drew first, so we guess he would be guilty."

Chapter 6

"I'll cut that big Adam's Apple outta your throat..."

The morning court session ended when Judge Jackson proclaimed Johnny Barton found guilty by a jury of his peers and the Judge issued a sentence of ten years in the state prison at Huntsville. With a bang of the gavel, the serving drinks began at the Cattlemen's Saloon prompting a rush by many to the bar and others making their way out to the various outhouses scattered around the small town to relieve strained bladders of the morning's whiskey. Promptly at one-thirty, the gavel banged again and the second trial began. The Sheriff directed a fourteen-year-old youth to run down the street to check on Deputy Washington bringing the prisoner to the courtroom.

While the Sheriff was busy entertaining the town's esteemed visitor with steaks for lunch and a few drinks at the Red-eye Saloon, and the personal attention of comely proprietor Betsy Brown, Deputy Washington had his hands full tending to the two prisoners. Johnny Barton was unwillingly returned to his jail cell amid a rash of cursing and slurs and struggling to break free of the chains that bound him. Washington had left the gunslinger chained and double-locked in his cell, and then he had to locate a second set of chains for the second prisoner Bobby Carroll.

Until this date, the Sheriff had managed the care of the two prisoners as they waited for their trial to be scheduled. Washington had been busy in his primary role as a hostler at the Bent Creek stable and he had been able to avoid contact with the man who had admitted lynching his sixteen-year-old son, Abraham Lincoln Washington, and when apprehended, Bobby Carroll had attempted to capture and lynch Washington as well. Only the intervention of Sheriff Holland had facilitated the capture of this murderer with deep racial hatred for folks who looked different than himself.

But, now on this date, with Washington again deputized and responsible for the care of the prisoners, and Bobby Carroll seeing that justice went against the young gunslinger, a like-minded fellow who had shared his attitudes and beliefs with his fellow prisoner, Bobby Carroll erupted in anger and determination to make a break for it. Bobby Carroll was a solidly built man who had done hard physical work when work was to be had, but mostly he had bounced around the west as a career outlaw who could never measure up to his younger brother Buck who was the ramrod for prominent rancher James Smith. Bobby Carroll knew he weighed more than the deputy, an aging fifty-something negro, and he was ready to fight to the death this day rather than be subjected to the humility of a public trial in the town where his brother lived and worked.

"Gimme those hands, both of them through the bars, so's I can get these irons on you." directed Washington.

"You come in here and just try to put 'em on me!" retorted prisoner Bobby Carroll.

Just then, Dennis McDonald, the 14-year-old son of rancher Donald McDonald, popped into the sheriff's office eager to help with bringing the prisoner to court. A slim gangly kid beginning a growth spurt, where he looked to be as tall a man but weighed half as much, he had an abundance of eager desire but likewise lacked an awareness of the danger the current circumstance presented.

Dennis saw Washington standing near the jail cell with the manacle chains and so he grabbed the jail keyring from the hook on the wall and walked over and opened the jail cell. Before he realized it, the young man was locked in the tight grasp of prisoner Carroll, with a sharpened spoon sticking in his throat, and a trickle of hot blood dripping down his chest staining his shirt.

21

"You're coming with me. Don't move or I'll cut that big Adam's Apple outta your throat." Bobby Carroll's deep growl sounded like a cougar and matched that of the seasoned predator that had pounced on a sheep and carried it off in one swift action.

Washington froze, seeing the immediate threat to the young man whose unthinking actions had stumbled into an already tense situation, now making it a life-threatening emergency. He backed away, putting space between them, yet moving towards the door to block their exit.

"Gun! Put your gun on that desk," barked Carroll. Washington remained frozen, blocking the exit. "Now, or I gut him like a fish!" Carroll jabbed the sharpened spoon again into the kid's throat causing him to gasp, and more blood flowed over the hand and down the shirt front.

Slowly, Washington reached for the pistol on his waist and slipped it on the desk, and then backed closer to the jail cells, but staying out of reach of Johnny Barton. "Let the boy go. Take me, it's really me you want," said Washington trying to find some way to save the scared boy.

"Get me outta here! Ya gotta spring me too," cried Barton, his voice high-pitched, sounding like a child crying.

"You not gonna get away. The town's full of people, they waiting for me to bring you, they gonna come looking any minute now." Washington hoped that he could stall Carroll so that the Sheriff might actually come for them. "He out there right now. I can see him," Washington lied.

Bobby Carroll's eyes darted from Washington to Barton, then to the gun on the desk and back to his rear. Standing behind the frightened kid, his right hand at the boy's throat, he reached for the Colt with his left hand, grabbed and cocked it, and pointed it at Washington.

"In the cell, get in the cell," Carroll yelled. Washington backed away slowly, his eyes searching for some solution while feeling his way back as directed. Carroll pulled the now crying boy to the door, leaned against it, and backed out. Slowly the prisoner and his hostage backed into the street. It was strangely quiet outside. Carroll pulled the kid around with the shiv at his throat, looking down the street. From somewhere a crow squawked a raucous caw as if seeking his attention. He tried desperately to ignore the bird as his eyes scanned the empty street, until settling on a man standing in the street in front of the Cattleman's Saloon, a crowd of people frozen behind him. It was

Sheriff Holland, legs spread shoulder width, standing tall, a head above the crowd of onlookers, right hand paused above the Colt hanging low on his belt.

"I ain't going to no lynchin'. I'm walking outta here. You try to stop me, and this boy gets gutted like a trout."

"Let him go, Carroll. Nobody's gonna die today." The Sheriff's voice was firm and calm and an echo bounced back from the stable at the end of the street.

Carroll, squeezed the shiv tighter to the throat of young Dennis as he held his hostage tightly and pulled them backward, step by step. The boy gagged and coughed, his feet stumbling trying to keep up, trying to keep from falling, trying to keep that shiv from cutting his throat once again. Slowly, they shuffled back toward the stable, there were horses in the stable.

"Bobby. Bobby, don't do this."

There was another voice. A voice he recognized, but it took a minute to sink in. Bobby Carroll continued to pull his hostage back to the horses, back to his escape.

"Bobby, don't do this. That boy don't deserve to die."

Then it hit him. Bobby recognized the voice. He scanned the crowd looking. Then there was a movement from the crowd, someone stepped out from behind the group of frozen silent onlookers.

"Leave me alone Buck, this ain't your fight."

"It ain't that boy's fight either Bobby. You always think you're so tough, but here you are again, hiding behind some innocent. You wanta end this? Step out here like a man."

"No! No! leave me alone! I'm getting outta here." Bobby's voice was higher pitched, faster, carrying uncontrolled fear.

"Let the boy go. Don't make me end it here." The Sheriff's voice was as calm as his stride was deliberate, closing the fifty yards that separated them, his Colt now centered on the anxious criminal's head.

Click-click.

It was the cock of a Winchester from off to Bobby's left. He turned to look over his shoulder. The pause in movement gave a larger target and the Sheriff thumbed the Colt. Suddenly, the young boy Dennis spun from his captor's grip, around falling -diving downward. Bobby tried to catch the boy and swing the shiv but it only caught air. There were two shots, close as an echo.

Seeing his brother in the sights of the Sheriff's Colt, Buck had lunged and slapped the gun downward causing the Sheriff's shot to harmlessly kick dirt in front of Bobby and his hostage. But, family love was not enough to protect his wayward brother from the long arm of the Texas law. The second show was the bang of the rifle, and in that delayed instant Bobby's eyes saw the big black hole of Winchester barrel, the yellow flash and smoke, and behind it the glare from the brown eyes of the negro deputy, and then nothing.

Chapter 7

"...we have the cure for what ails you."

It was a crisp sunny morning with a scattering of white puffs floating overhead, giving a feeling of a new beginning, moving forward past the trial, and the hostage incident. The drifter Bobby Carroll who had taken the young hostage in an escape try had been shot dead by deputy Washington, had been quietly buried in a far corner of the vast Smith ranch as an accommodation to brother Buck Carroll who had a sound reputation as the ramrod for the Smith Ranch. And fast-gun Johnny Barton, a former Smith Ranch hand had been taken off to the state prison at Huntsville escorted by Deputy Washington and Judge Jackson who traveled as far as San Antonio.

The early risers who ventured forth in town this morning found various colorful posters displayed about town on the sides of buildings and on the pillars of the porticos and porch overhangs. One man heading towards the Cattleman's stopped to look, his attention drawn to the brightly colored message proclaiming:

Miracle Medicine

Dr. Jeremiah Jacobs invents modern elixir –

The proven cure for aches, pains, and maladies.

Medicine Show today 10:00 AM sharp.

Soon others came along and stopped to look and read the posters. Another poster had been placed on the corner of McCann's Mercantile, showed the drawing of a man standing at the back of a colorful wooden wagon holding up a bottle as a crowd gathered, over the message that read:

Jacobs Wizard Oil - a modern elixir
Eliminate aches pains, and maladies
Limited supply-Get yours today- 10:00 AM Sharp.

"Good morning Miss Betsy, I'm famished. What's cooking this morning?" asked the Sheriff as he walked into the Red-eye.

"Steak and eggs, just the way you like it, Clay," said Betsy as she swished up in her red dress, petticoats, and a big smile, a cup of coffee in hand for her favorite customer.

"Why you're lookin' bright-eyed and bushy-tailed," said the Sheriff as he accepted the hot coffee and settled into what seemed to be his reserved seat back near the kitchen. He held the white ceramic cup between both hands warming his fingers from the morning chill. A wisp of steam rose from the hot beverage bringing with it that welcoming aroma of the coffee. The Sheriff inhaled the bouquet of the beverage and recognized its added ingredient, flavoring to his taste preferences. He winked in appreciation to his blonde hostess.

"I know your likes and dislikes and how to satisfy your appetite and that your coffee comes with a splash of bourbon," said Betsy.

She always savored their time together and looked for unspoken ways to show her interest. Their friendship seemed to be evolving, subtly towards a closer casual familiarity, perhaps unrecognized by the Sheriff who still considered himself in mourning over the loss of his wife Sarah killed four years ago by a stage robber. But in the past year, the Sheriff had trailed and attempted to bring in the man who had murdered his wife; the man had elected to fight to the death rather than allow his capture. Since that time, Clay had seemed to warm up to the coquettish entreaties from the attractive owner of the Red-eye.

"So what's the excitement outside," she asked as she brought out his steak and eggs cooked to perfection and sat down with a cup of coffee.

"Well, it looks like some feller who calls himself Doctor Jacobson has some miracle cure for all that ails us and he'll be offering it to the fine folks of Bent Creek later this morning."

"Maybe I should stop by and see what he is offering," commented Betsy.

"If I may say so, Miss Betsy, you already have what cures any ails of a man, with your fine cooking and your fine establishment here."

"Why Clay, you embarrass me so," she said with a flush to her cheeks that matched her red dress.

"Sheriff! Sheriff Holland, that man's disrupting my business. He's parked that wagon right in front of my store. My customers can't get in or out without that man haranguing at them at my front door." It was Harold McCann, all in a huff about the traveling medicine man who stopped his wagon right in front of the general store.

"What? You afraid of a little competition?" laughed the Sheriff, as he glanced at Betsy and winked.

"My customers can't even get in my store, and that man's stopping them and taking their money. I won't have it. Not at my front door!" Spittle flew and McCann's face was getting redder as his voice rose.

"One of my girls asked for part of the day off at ten so that she could attend his presentation," said Betsy. "Sounds like he's getting an early start."

"Well, Harold, let's go have a talk with this feller," said the Sheriff, as he took a final swig of coffee and set the cup down along with some coins to pay for breakfast. "Thank ya, dear. Mighty fine as usual. You never disappoint."

As the Sheriff and Harold McCann walked out of the Red-eye, they could already see a crowd gathering in front of McCann's store, surrounding a one-horse rig wood wagon, with what appeared to be a tiny house on top, all painted in bright colors. The wagon and the wooden structure above were painted a weathered yellow, with large red lettering reading " Dr. Jeremiah Jacobs Patent Medicine – Jacobs Wizard Oil – Modern Elixer – cures all ills." There was a picture of a brown bottle with a narrow top and bright label and a picture of a smiling man with a beard.

As they walked up to the crowd, they could see a tall rail-like man head and shoulders above the group of townspeople. He stepped up onto a small porch at the back of his wagon, now looking strangely impressive with a thick curly dark beard wearing a stiff white shirt with string tie under a wool suit with a stovepipe hat, a stature that likely would tower over the nation's assassinated president who stood at six feet four. The rail-thin man with the tall hat now resembled a stick figure drawn by a child. Comic looks aside, the man began talking in a light friendly banter, in a pleasant voice that carried out some thirty-forty feet without seeming to shout.

"Good morning on this beautiful day,…step right up, yes ma'am, ladies and children too, step right up and learn about the benefits of Jacobs Wizard Oil – the modern elixir, a patent medicine, to which I, Jeremiah Jacobs, invented and hold the patent granted by the United States Patent Office in Washington DC. Do you have an aching back or sore arms? Are you pained by arthritis or stiff joints? Do you suffer from constipation or digestive disorders or the runs?" He held up the little brown bottle as he talked nodding to one person, and a small wave to another as he caught their eye.

People were stepping closer, nodding to themselves, or speaking quietly to the person next to them acknowledging that they had experienced one or more of the maladies described. A woman with two shall children inched closer to the group of interested observers.

"Yessiree, Good morning there, sir, ma'am. Those are fine-looking children there. You're just in time, we have the cure for what ails you. There are still a few bottles left---"

"Pardon me there Mr. Jacobs, but your poster says that the show begins at ten," the Sheriff spoke loudly and strongly like in the old days when one Ranger was sent to quell one riot. "And, well, here we are well before that time, and furthermore—"

"Well kind sir, we have an anxious crowd here in this lovely town. It's Benda Creek, is that right? Well, I will not disappoint—" The man with the smooth voice continued his patter as if there were no interruption.

The Sheriff interrupted again, this time louder. "I am Sheriff Clay Holland, and Mr. Jacob, you are a guest in my town, subject to my rules. And your wagon is blocking access to the McCann Merchandising store right here. You're going to have to move down the way so that you don't disrupt the other merchants here in town." The Sheriff's volume grew louder with each sentence spoken. If you don't move this little wagon back another one hundred feet, I will shut you down."

"Of course, kind sir, we are happy to oblige, just as soon as I give this quick demonstration —"

"I'll smack that horse's ass and that trailer will move with or without you." The Sheriff had his gun in the air and he took step towards the horse. The tooth-pick man was suddenly walking alongside the sheriff moving quickly back to the horse, where he released the brake and walked the animal down another hundred feet. He set the brake and climbed up to the small stage at the back of the wagon once again beginning his spiel as the crowd followed closely along.

A man had stepped up to the stage, he appeared to be limping and held up his hand weakly as if reaching for the little brown bottle. "Oh, it hurts. Doctor,…Doctor Jacobs, I want to buy your medicine."

"Now you, sir, a moment ago, you told me that you were experiencing a condition called lumbar neuritis. Poor sir, you've injured your back." Dr. Jacobs looked down at the man with an exaggerated expression of concern, holding the little brown bottle just out of reach.

The man grimaced and moaned, as he reached again, then let out a hoarse cough.

Dr. Jacobs continued, "A lifting incident. Happens to us all; was it a bale of hay, a saddle, hoisting a load as a teamster? I have just what you need, Jacobs Wizard Oil. It will eliminate aches and pains. And I hear that cough. My, my, it's lucky you found our wagon. That sounds like the croup. Potentially contagious, if not properly medicated." The man coughed and reached again for the little bottle.

"For a mere one dollar. Jacobs Wizard Oil. Please sir one dollar. I only have a few bottles left." The man handed up a dollar and twisted the cap and swallowed the contents of the medicine.

"Ah, oh my, halleluiah! I feel better already." The man stretched and did a deep bend to touch his toes. "Oh, thank you, Doctor Jacobs. Thank you so much." The man walked away. Others crowded forward. Many waved a dollar in their hand trying to get the doctor's attention.

Sheriff Holland watched the show now from the plank walkway a few yards behind the crowd that had gathered, and eagerly followed as the wagon was moved away from the front of McCann's store. I've seen these shows before, he thought. Miracle medicine my ass! I still prefer the bourbon that Sam sells over at the Cattleman's. Now, that man there, that first one to buy, thought the Sheriff, he's not from around here; I recollect I saw him climbing down from the stage a day or two ago.

"Just a few left. One at a time, please. Have your dollar ready, here you are sir. One dollar, thank you." Dr. Jacobs, a twinkle in his eye, was efficiently handling the crowd of anxious people, each hoping for a miracle cure from the daily aches and pains of life on the Texas prairie. "And you ma'am one dollar for yours'. Here you are. Who's next, please? Step right up. Have your dollar ready. Just one each please until we are sure there are enough to go around. One dollar. Here you are. Thank you, kind sir."

Chapter 8

"Damn thief! You come around here again, I'll get you."

The show on Main street was just the perfect distraction for one person in Bent Creek. He watched from a distance, in the shadows, down an alley behind McCann's Mercantile. He saw the Sheriff and another man, the merchant, walking from the Red-eye towards the throng gathered around the funny stick man in the brightly painted wagon. The funnyman talked fast and he held their interest. Even the other merchants had come out from their stores and places of business to watch the show. This was his opportunity, like the boss, the *jefe* had said. He had to move quickly.

First, the store, in the back door. There were so many things here, so much to choose from, it is a paradise for the pickings. Only one time before had he been in a store like this with his mother. A Colt from under the counter, oh, it's heavy. For the gun he must have bullets, looking, he found a box of 44-40. That looked right. Outside now, the sheriff's voice, oh good, he's making the medicine man move his wagon. His search continued, now, a shirt, pants, and over in this corner next to a bench, shoes. These look about right. Wait! Look there, in that jar on the counter, hard candies, peppermints, and lemon drops for the little ones. Voices! The merchant is coming. He struggled to hold all his prizes and ran out the back door.

It was exciting, these finds. Especially on days like this. Not just grabbing one item from some lonely ranch house and running. The pick of a store like this was like a day in heaven. To have so much stuff was just unbelievable. When you grow up poor and have to work in the fields to receive a few coins or some ears of corn or scraps from a table, you become thankful to just bring home a scrap to mama to be shared with the little brothers and sisters. And you hope that Papa's not home when you come in, because if he catches you with the prize of your daily labor, he takes it and goes to the cantina for whiskey. So, you hide it from Papa so that the little ones can have something to eat.

Papa was gone most of the time, and the few times he came around, he smelled of cigarillos and whiskey and the little ones would hide because he sounded so mean and angry. As the oldest, Tomas tried to protect the little ones from papa's explosive "*enfado*," sometimes enduring a beating. But when Tomas' hand was accidentally cut by a farmer trying to harvest agave, Papa had tied off the severed limb saving the boy's life, at the cost of a lost left hand.

Then, one day not long ago, Mama had come home crying, saying that Papa had died. Papa died because he had been in a fight at the cantina, a fight with guns. Now twelve years old, he was the man of the family, even with only one hand and a stump at his left wrist, he could do most things and carry his weight on a job. He was now working for the jefe, like this job on the north side of Rio Bravo; he would bring things to the jefe, and he would get his cut, and bring prizes home to mama.

He ran back into a copse of live oak trees and dropped his bootie, and then circled around the buildings to the back of the saloon called Red-eye. There was activity there, where a cook was in and out of the door several times, working a well-pump, and throwing out some trash. A mongrel dog hung out there waiting for scraps. The dog saw him and growled, baring its teeth. He hated to compete with animals for food because they were alert to the intrusion and such fierce fighters protecting their find. He decided to move down the way to the other saloon. It was quieter there, not so much activity. An older woman came in and out once, and then again, and then it was quiet.

He decided to try his luck at the back door. He snuck up close to the door, snuck along the back wall, and listened. Inside were voices, men's voices, and the clink of glasses. There were talk and some laughter; he counted three voices, three men. The woman was now silent or perhaps she had gone somewhere else. He got close to the doorway and peeked inside. The back room was now empty and quiet. It had the look of a kitchen, but not as big or busy as the place down the way. There was a storeroom, like a pantry, and some vegetables. He moved quickly, grabbed a handful of potatoes and a loaf of bread, and started for the door. There just inside on a small shelf was a bottle of whiskey. He grabbed the bottle and bolted for the door.

"Hey! What you doing there? Get outta here!" a man's voice yelled. "Damn thief! You come around again, I'll get you!"

The sneak-thief ran around behind the stable and followed a creek bed into a wooded area. He didn't stop until he had circled back to the wooded copse of trees where he had stashed the bootie from the store. Where was his partner? They were supposed to meet here as soon as they were finished. He hid behind a bush, waiting, watching. He guessed that ten or twenty- minutes had passed.

After a while, he was getting hungry. So many times before he had known hunger. But now he had some food, there was plenty to share. He knew he was supposed to bring the bootie back to share with the others, but now his stomach was growling. Besides, he still had the candy for the kids. Bring the candy, it would make him a hero in the eyes of the others. He pulled at the bread, for just a little bite. The bread was good, but it made him thirsty. The creek was back on the other side of the roadway, too far to go without being seen.

The bottle of whiskey! That was supposed to be for the jefe, but he could just have a little sip, nobody would know. He pulled off the cork and it smelled sweet. He had seen papa with a whiskey bottle, carrying it around, keeping it close at hand, lifting it up to his lips, and tipping his head back as he took a big swallow and wiped his lips with a sleeve. Just like papa, he put the bottle to his lips and leaned back for a big swallow. The liquid splashed down his throat faster than he expected causing him to choke as some dribbled down his chin. It was fiery hot, causing him to blow hard to try to put out the burning wetness in his throat.

Now, he heard a dog barking. No, there were two dogs. It seemed like they were coming his way. Maybe the store owner or the saloon owner were coming after him, tracking him with dogs. *Jefe* always said don't mess with dogs or coyotes or the big cats. They attack and bite, they'll fight you for food, and they can track you, follow you by your smell. The barking was getting close, and there were men's voices, yelling, winded like they were running. His heart was now pounding.

The dogs barked louder; they were getting nearer. He grabbed his bootie, struggling to hold everything, the food, the gun, the clothes, and the candy, but it fell, there was too much to carry in his hands. Panic sharpens the mind and devises solutions. Quickly, he tied knots in the pant legs and stuffed his bootie into the pants from the top, the food in one leg, and the clothing and gun in the other leg. He pulled the top tight with a bandana and began to run with his funny-looking parcel.

Tomas ran further into the woods, then downhill towards the creek bed. The *jefe* had said that if you are pursued, run through the creeks, up-stream or down, because the dogs can't track your smell in the moving water, and then stay in the water for a while and come out where the ground is rocky or hard and leaves no tracks. He had learned to listen to the jefe because the jefe was wise to the ways of the world. He had seen what had happened to another boy who had not followed the jefe's instructions. The boy had been captured and sent away to jail. The water was cold, it numbed his feet, and the rocks in the stream were slippery. Once he fell, but managed to hold up his prize, as he tumbled into the water getting soaked, a difficult task with but one hand. But he had managed to keep his prize up in the air; he didn't want the bullets or the bread or the candy to get wet.

Now he ran, cold and shivering and wet, but the dogs seemed farther away. He would go to the alternate meeting place, near the tree the jefe called the hanging tree. He would hide there and wait for the *jefe*.

Chapter 9

...shunned by others, he covered his face...

Manuel Chavez, the *abuelo* or grandfather, nudged his sorrel into a lope as he passed over the ridge and back down into a dry wash, trying to minimize any profile that could be spotted from a distance. The dark blonde animal had been a real find, captured by one of his followers in Laredo on the southern fringe of the area that he considered his territory. This animal was a good reliable runner, a horse that took to the trail and loved a good workout while expecting little of the comforts of those animals that had become lazy in the remudas working on the ranches in Texas.

Today, he was going to check on followers working in the area along the northern headlands of the Nueces River. Things were coming together nicely, after a difficult start. He still remembered that day, that early morning rustle of cattle from the Smith herd, catching them asleep with only two-night riders, the gunshots, the startled stampede southward; he had taken the lead, steering the running cows. Just when they came off the ridge down into the valley of Rio Bravo, the gringos had managed to catch up, forming and executing a counter-attack to reclaim the herd. As he looked back now, he had to give them credit for their last stand strategy of taking out the leader and turning the herd just before they reached the fording point across the river.

He was the leader, and he should have seen it coming, but he didn't. The river was just ahead, the thirsty animals smelled water and followed as he led them to the ford, only to be set upon by their vicious surprise attack. Somehow, he had managed to survive, his horse being shot and stumbling, sending him into the dirt as the hundreds of animals charged overhead. He had somehow managed to hide under his bloodied dying struggling mount, in the pathway towards the ford. But the dying horse, the smell of blood, the shots, and the shouts of the gringos had been determined and had turned the herd back up the ridge and away from the river.

The *abuelo* had not survived unscathed. His injuries had been a setback, injuries causing him to be shunned by others. So, he covered his face and had built a new life now doing what he did best, using his wiles to take from others their property or animals or money. But now, he had new helpers, a *pandilla de hijos*, a gang of children, those children of the streets, who he found as he worked the streets and roads on both sides of Rio Bravo. His new followers were children who had run away from home or been orphaned or had been abandoned because a destitute parent had been unable or unwilling to care for a child stricken with some kind of physical malady.

He considered his prize *seguidor* or follower, young Tomas, a twelve-year-old who had lost his left hand in an agave harvesting accident but was trying to find odd jobs to help support his overworked mother and four siblings. He was going today to see what Tomas and another young *seguidor* had accomplished after being dropped off three days ago near the town of Bent Creek. They were to meet by the hanging tree, a large old cottonwood on the east side of town, a tree that had been so dubbed because it had been used as a hanging tree the year before.

The gray clouds were high and the light wind blew from the west. As he rode northward, a hawk circled overhead soaring in the breeze high above. Then he heard the bark of a perrito de las praderas, a prairie dog, warning others in their family of the hawk's presence overhead. The animals scurried into their burrows in the ground. The *abuelo* bypassed a *pueblo de las praderas,* a prairie dog town, noting its location in case they needed to catch some of the little brown rodents if other wildlife were not found for food.

Up ahead, lie the roadway between San Antonio and Bent Creek, and off to the left was the stand of cottonwoods including the large tree now dubbed by locals as the hanging tree. Stories are spread by travelers and the story of the hanging of a negro youth had made its way into the pueblos and cantinas south of Rio Bravo. The hanging tree was a natural landmark that revealed itself from nearly a quarter-mile away. The *abuelo* approached cautiously, wary of travelers on this main east-west roadway. Perhaps it was not the best choice for a meeting point; a passing traveler may have come upon the *niño abandonado,* a waif and taken him along on their journey. But, the *seguidores* were always instructed to stay out of sight.

The *abuelo* tied his horse to a sapling off the trail, and he began to circle the area by foot staying under the cover of bushes and tall bunchgrass. After one circle, approximately fifty yards out from the stand of cottonwoods with no observation of the young *seguidor*, the *abuelo* mimicked the song of the white-winged dove, waited, and gave a second series of hooting coos. From behind, there was a similar coo. Hiding behind a fiddlewood bush, the *abuelo* tossed a tiny pebble in the direction of the other coo, but no bird was flushed to the air. Rather, a similar pebble landed in his direction.

"¿Tomas, Dónde estás?" Tomas, where are you? It was a loud whisper.

"Aquí estoy." Here I am. There was a rustling in the bushes and in a moment Tomas appeared in a crouch walk sneaking towards the *jefe.*

"¿Qué tienes para mí?" What do you have for me? The *abuelo's* voice was quietly stern, his eyes scanning the area around the boy for his stolen prizes.

"Por allí, escondido en los arbustos." Over there, hidden in the bushes. The boy held his ground, unafraid of the sternness of the *jefe.* He led the *jefe* in a circuitous route to a thick bunch of the fiddlewood, to a stash of his bootie taken from the store and the saloon in Bent Creek. The *jefe* rummaged through the bootie, quickly finding the colt, then digging for the bullets, and then finding the whiskey. He took a swig and wiped his lips on his sleeve. Noticing the young *seguidor* watching him, he offered the boy a tear-off of bread and a swig of water from his canteen.

"Está bien, lo hiciste bien, joven." It is good, you did well, young man. The *jefe* kept a stern countenance but inside, he was pleased with the efforts of his young *seguidor*. He licked his lips savoring again the bite of the whiskey.

"¿Donde esta su compañero, Santiago?" Where is your partner, Santiago?

"No lo sé. Yo no lo he visto." I don't know, I have not seen him, the twelve-year-old replied.

"*Esto está bien escondido, vamos a buscarlo.*" This is well hidden, let's go find him. The *abuelo* led his *seguidor* out of the thick bushes and back to his horse. They mounted and rode double northwards towards the sheep ranch. Last year, he had rustled part of the sheep flock, and the second *seguidor* had been sent to find other treasures from the sheep rancher.

As usual, the *abuelo* stayed off the trail, riding in a parallel direction several hundred yards to the east in the draws and arroyos. They rode in silence for a while, alert to the terrain, and watching for Santiago.

After a while, the twelve-year-old asked a question. "*Jefe, ¿por qué llevas esa mascara?*" Boss, why do you wear that mask? The *abuelo* had always worn the mask since the boy had begun working for him. Until now, he had not dared to ask about it. But now, seeing that the *jefe* was pleased with the bootie, the boy was emboldened.

"*¿Esa Mascara? Es porque, como tú, tengo un lesion pero en la cara.*" That mask? It is because, like you, I have an injury, but to my face. The *jefe* touched the white silk mask with eye and mouth slots that covered his face.

His mind recalled the events that had led to his wearing the mask, the stampede, and the shot that had felled his horse on that final approach to the river. The first few animals had stumbled over his fallen mount and had trampled his body and his face, causing him to lose two fingers on his left hand, and to have his face mangled and so disfigured that no beard could cover the ugliness. He had crawled back to his shanty in the Piedras Negras region but found that women caregivers winced and turned away to avoid looking at his scrambled egg face, while little children screamed and ran away from the *fantasma feo*, the ugly ghost. Only when a visiting priest had left a white silk hood cut with eye holes to cover his ugliness, had he then been able to move about the village without scaring the women and children.

Chapter 10

...spreading the fire, creating a line of flames...

"Veo las ovejas." I see the sheep, said the *abuelo*. There were a few strays, and then a flock of the animals. The *abuelo* steered his sorrel through a low wash around to the upwind side of the animals. *"Tranquilo. Velemos por el pastor."* Quiet. We watch for the shepherd.

Alert to the presence of others, the *abuelo* kept his distance and watched silently for a few moments. Here was a small flock, maybe a hundred animals watched by a young man just a year or two older than Tomas. Soon, there was a cooing sound like that of a white-winged dove. The *abuelo* looked around and, not seeing any birds in the air or in the scattering of nearby trees, he answered with the same call. From their left, Santiago appeared from behind a bunch of mesquite. They dismounted and walked back towards Santiago and the cover of the bushes. The *abuelo* gestured to his two young *seguidores* to talk quietly.

"¿Cuantas ovejas aqui?" How many sheep here? the *abuelo* asked.

"Un cien." One hundred, Santiago replied, then pointed towards the north. *"Pero hay mil en el campo por el rancho."* But there are a thousand in the field by the ranch.

"¿Hay otros premios, otros animales?" Are there other prizes? Other animals?

"Sí, hay un caballo de reyes." Yes, there is a horse of kings. There was excitement in Santiago's voice.

The *abuelo* quieted his two young *seguidores* and gave them instructions. They quickly set about following the instruction. Santiago, who normally walked with a limp because of an injured foot, circled around closer to the herd and then began limping exaggeratedly and falling like he was injured, attracting the attention of the shepherd. As the shepherd approached, Santiago stumbled and fell and remained down like he was unconscious. The young shepherd, surprised to see someone so far from town, walked over concerned about what had happened to the child who appeared to have fallen and couldn't get up. Just as he leaned over the inert body on the ground, Tomas appeared from behind and whacked the shepherd on the back of the head with a fist-sized stone. Santiago began leading the flock of sheep southward, while the *abuelo* pulled Tomas up behind the saddle and they headed northward towards the sheep ranch.

As soon as the *abuelo* saw the sheep ranch in the distance, he circled the sorrel around up-wind, dismounted behind a small rise, and positioned behind a mesquite bush to watch the activity and locate the horse of kings. There it was, in a corral behind the small barn, a beautiful animal. Even from several hundred yards away he could see its fine lines and its markings. It was shiny black with a white star forehead and four white stockings. The animal looked so out of place on this tiny sheep ranch on the prairie. It had a finely chiseled head, a long arching neck, and a high tail position. It truly was a horse of kings. Young Santiago had done well in finding and reporting this prize.

He watched a while longer, checking the activities of the people, the animals, the dogs, and especially the activity of the fine-looking shiny black horse. He looked back towards where Santiago had taken the small flock of sheep and begun driving them back southward. They were out of sight, and he wanted to give them time to move from the area. He would need to create a diversion. He came up with a plan and described the plan to young Tomas giving specific instructions.

Tomas's eyes twinkled in excitement as he nodded in eager anticipation of this new assignment by the *jefe*. He was anxious to please and would do his best. He crouched and ran in the direction as instructed. He found a dead mesquite bush, some dried bunch grass, and even some dried tumbleweed. Perfect. Tomas circled farther, found a dip, and lit the match putting it to the dried bunchgrass creating a small handheld torch. Then he began to light the grassy areas and move back towards the starting point where the *jefe* waited. Midway he came back upon the dried mesquite and the tumbleweed. The breeze was picking up now, and the flames were beginning to take hold and blow towards the flock of sheep. Now he lit the tumbleweed and tossed it into the air letting the breeze catch it and pull it through the bunchgrasses in the field quickly spreading the fire and creating a line of flames and the moving flames were now beginning to separate the flock from the ranch.

Within moments, Tomas heard the bays of the sheep as the small animals now smelled the smoke and saw the blowing line of flames. Then he heard the voices, shouting, as the sheep rancher and his workers were suddenly aware of the flames moving towards the sheep and separating the sheep from the ranch. The animals were panicking and running, making a baying sound of fear. Tomas ran toward where the *jefe* waited, but he didn't see the old man with the white silk mask. Behind, he heard a horse, but before he could turn around, he was scooped up by strong hands and swung to the horse's galloping rump.

The sorrel charged toward the corral behind the barn, leaped the top rail, and followed the leads of the expert horseman where he was reigned in when the shiny black animal was spotted.

"*Abra la Puerta y monta para conocer a Santiago.* Open the gate and ride to meet Santiago, said the *abuelo*. "*Continuar hacia el sur. Estaré a lo largo pronto.*" Continue to the south. I'll be along soon.

As Tomas rode out the gate, he heard the *jefe*, his voice now sounding very calm, speaking to the horse of kings.

Chapter 11

"They attacked my property again,…stole my prize Arabian."

Sheep rancher Donald McDonald was butchering a sheep for dinner, taking advantage of one of the prerogatives of all ranchers, the ability to select the day's dinner on the hoof, and serve fresh meat to family and ranch hands. Focusing on the task at hand, he failed to immediately notice the circumstances that prompted his flock to bay in panic and begin a fearful stampede to avoid a fire that was now raging in his pasture. His attention was finally diverted when the sheepdog began barking and several ranch hands heard the animals, finally noticing the oncoming flames and blowing smoke. One wing of the flames was headed toward the ranch buildings, while part of the fire had panicked the flock. The hands ran towards the fire.

The blowing smoke had caused the horses including the Arabian, in the corral to become nervous. The show horse was calmed by the smooth soft voice of the strange handler who stroked his neck and offered a treat. In just a moment, the stranger had a saddle on the animal and lead him away from the fearful smell of the smoke in the air. The Arabian did not contest when the calm stranger mounted and confidently guided the animal out to fresh air and freedom.

In the field south of the McDonald sheep ranch, shepherd Dennis McDonald, the 14-year-old son of rancher Donald McDonald, was finally waking up from a hard knock to the head. The back of his head ached, and when he reached back, there was some blood and matted hair around a large swollen knot. He sat up slowly, tried to stand, but stumbled, still dizzied by the knock on the head, and sat back down again for a few minutes. After a few minutes, he tried to stand again.

Then, Dennis looked around, searching for the flock that he was tending, and looking for the young boy that had appeared to be hobbling in the field and fell down. The boy was gone, and the flock was gone. He thought that he had seen a horse and rider calmly riding towards town. He looked in a wide circle of the prairie and saw nothing until his eyes surveyed north towards the family ranch when he saw smoke in the air blowing across the fields. Then he could hear distant voices and smell the smoke from the burning grass. Slowly, he began walking back toward the ranch.

Later that day, after having controlled the fire and collected the fleeing flock, Donald MacDonald took his son into the town on the wagon, to have him checked by Doc and to report the fire, the theft of the small flock of one hundred animals, and the missing and presumed theft of his prized Arabian show horse.

Considered to be a prominent citizen in Bent Creek, Doc was a former civil war medic for the confederacy who learned most of his skills behind the lines in make-shift tents where wounded soldiers were given seat-of-the-pants medical care and field surgery without the benefit of anesthetic. He had been conscripted for this assignment during the unit's first engagement because he had demonstrated some first aid skills for wounded fellow soldiers on the battlefield. The moniker had stuck and it became his occupation when he returned to West Texas at the end of the war.

MacDonald left his son with Doc for an examination of the knock on the head, while he went searching for the Sheriff. His first stop was at the sheriff's office, and then at the Cattleman's Saloon but not finding him at either place. By the time he arrived at his third stop, the Red-eye Saloon, his temper was boiling over.

"Sheriff Holland! While you're in here lazing over lunch or dinner or drinks, my property has been attacked again, my son assaulted, my sheep stolen, and my ranch set ablaze. And my prize Arabian is gone. I'm sure that they set the fire to take my prize horse." Spittle flew as MacDonald loomed over the sheriff while he sat at a table having lunch. Other patrons stopped their eating and drinking, watching the angry display. Betsy and her cook stepped out from the kitchen to see what the commotion was all about.

"It must be that Texas tornado blowing off the prairies," said the Sheriff with a smirk, as he recognized the excited voice while calmly sipping a whiskey. "Why don't you set a spell and tell me what's going on?"

The sheep rancher was so wound up that he walked in tight circles, arms flailing, repeating his claim, "They,…they attacked my property again, set a fire, stole my sheep and assaulted my son, stole my sheep. And, and I'm sure that they stole my prize Arabian!"

"You're dancing like there's ants in your pants." The Sheriff stood and matched the excited man eye to eye, grabbed his shoulders, and pushed him down into a seat. "Betsy get our excited friend a whiskey."

Mac Donald finally accepted a drink, took a breath, and told the story one more time answering the questions raised by the Sheriff. After a few minutes, Doc came into the Red-eye with the young Mac Donald. "This here youngin's got a bit to add to the story. Tell the Sheriff what you told me."

Dennis MacDonald described what had happened to him in the field, that he had seen an injured boy who had fallen, and when he walked over to check on what had happened, he was hit from behind. Then, when he awoke, he saw that the sheep were gone and that he saw a rider on a horse going towards town.

"Tell 'em what he looked like. Tell 'em what you told me," prompted Doc.

"Well, I'm not sure, after that hit on the head, I thought I was dreaming or something. There was this, this ghost riding a horse down the pathway, a horse that looked like the Arabian." The young Mac Donald shrugged his shoulders like he wasn't sure what he was saying.

"A ghost?" Are you nuts?" The older Mac Donald, getting excited again was on his feet standing over his son who flinched and backed away fearful of a strike.

The Sheriff grabbed the excited father and pushed him back into the chair. "Now son, just tell me what you saw. Why did you call it a ghost?"

"It,…it looked like a ghost, with a silky white face just riding along minding its own business."

Betsy and the girls were laughing in the background by the kitchen. The Sheriff gestured to them to quiet down and back away. "Silky white? The whole thing was silky white? Say what you saw, man."

The boy repeated, "I saw a man riding the Arabian, but he had a silky white face, made me think it was a ghost."

"How did the horse behave," queried the Sheriff. He added, "I've seen horses get spooked out in *llano estacado* at a Comanche spirit site, won't go near it. How was the horse?"

"Calm as could be, just trotting along at a smooth lope."

"It's gotta be that *Bandido Fantasma*, my ghost bandit." Texas Ranger Bonner O'Toole had just come in and joined the conversation. "There was kids, you say?"

"Well, before, then I was hit on the head, and then I saw that ghost ruder," said the young MacDonald. "I didn't think that the kid was with the rider."

"Let's just put the pieces together, youngin'." The Ranger had center floor now. "If I'm hearing all the parts of your story, one, you saw a kid who seemed injured and you went to help, two, you get bushwacked on the back of the head, and three, when you awake, the flock is gone, and four, this ghost looking feller is riding away on a fine horse belonging to your pappy? Am I right?"

Young Dennis MacDonald nodded. "Yes sir, that sounds right."

A crowd of others had congregated in the Red-eye now listening to the events. Just then, Harold McCann, proprietor of McCann's Mercantile stepped forward and joined the discussion. "I was robbed also, happened when that medicine man was in town, setting up shop right in front of my store. Remember, sheriff, when we made him move because of all the people on the porch blocking my door? Well, I've since discovered I have missing merchandise, a Colt, box of shells, shoes, and some clothes. I thought it might a been that medicine man."

"Well, we moved him down to clear your doorway, and near as I could tell, he was in or on his wagon the whole time," replied the Sheriff. "Seems highly unlikely he robbed you. He didn't come into the store, did he?"

"No, he didn't," said McCann. "But there were some ladies and some children about that time."

"Any un-escorted children?" asked the Ranger.

"Now that I recall, might have been," conceded the merchant, adding. "Some of the neighborhood dogs was getting pretty excited about that time."

The Ranger turned to the Sheriff, "well my friend, the ghost bandit is working in the area and he has just struck in Bent Creek."

Chapter 12

All activity in the saloon froze as others watched...

The Sheriff and Ranger Bonner O'Toole had ridden out to the MacDonald sheep ranch first thing in the morning after learning about the assault on young Dennis MacDonald, the range fire, and the theft of sheep and the prize Arabian horse. It all seemed to be connected and Ranger O'Toole was convinced that it was the handiwork of the man they called the ghost bandit. MacDonald led the grand tour showing off the improvements he had made since acquiring the property a year before from homesteaders.

The highlight, of course, was the burnt grassland that had consumed one outbuilding, a storage shed, for tools and equipment, and the stable area where the Arabian had been kept. It was nearing the end of winter and spring was just around the corner, so much of the burnt prairie was expected to recover and likely thrive because prairie fires are a common outcome of spring thunderstorms. It was just nature's way of renewing the land and the soil. The Sheriff did find a sheltered area in the cover of a copse of cottonwoods along a nearby creek bed. It showed the ingenuity that the young thief had used to make a natural shelter and survive during a period of observing the sheep ranch operations. The Sheriff surmised that the missing hundred sheep or so had not made a big dent in MacDonald's flock because he had a thousand or more across the ranch. The loss of the Arabian, of course, was the man's main gripe because that was his prize animal.

"As we discussed before if you recall," the Sheriff reminded the sheep rancher, "our ability to track and capture un-branded sheep is difficult. In the day or two since the theft, those animals likely have been marched across the river and disappeared into thirty or more family flocks of Mexican peasants. Now, that Arabian, that's another story. That's a fine animal, people will recognize it and we can trail that animal and any reports of its presence."

"Just get him back as fast as you can. I'd hate to think of someone who would hurt that fine animal or treat him unjustly."

"Mr. MacDonald, my orders from the Ranger Captain are to work this area and capture the one they call *Bandido Fantasma,*" said Ranger O'Toole. "That he is on that fine horse makes my job all the more easier. Rest assured, we'll get our man."

On return to Bent Creek, The Sheriff and Ranger O'Toole stopped in at the Cattleman's Saloon to wash away the trail dust. Bartender Sam set their whiskeys on the bar in response to an unspoken nod from the Sheriff. A quick swallow by each emptied their glasses, followed by a refill gesture, this time from the Ranger. Their eyes drifted around the saloon keeping track of the patrons engaged in quiet talk while the card came led by dealer Leverett Brockton III had a group of four quietly considering their hands and fingering their respective pots.

After a few minutes, a stranger walked in, paused at the door to give the place a once-over, and then stepped up to the end of the bar farthest away from where the law-men stood. Sam went down to the end of the bar to take his order.

"What'll it be?"

"You got that Tennessee whiskey,…Jack Daniels?" The man spoke with confidence like he expected special service. He was tall, nearly six feet, hair slicked back, and dressed all spiffy in store a bought dark gray woolen suit with white pinstripes, looking kinda like a St. Louis gambler.

"That's premium stuff, I got standard stock, cost a lot less." Sam glanced at the lawmen like he anticipated trouble.

"I'll take the premium stuff, buy the bottle if I have to." It was apparent that the spiffy stranger was used to getting his way regardless of cost.

Sheriff Clay Holland caught the nuances of the conversation and turned to face the stranger. His glance took a measure of the man, the fine clothes, the confident insistence for premium whiskey. An instinctive evaluation observed no obvious presence of a heavy Colt on his hip, but the gambler look of him suggested he likely kept a pocket pistol hidden but available.

A gold piece clinked on the bar to back up the stranger's demand. Sam pulled up a bottle of the Tennessee whiskey and began to un-cork it. "I keep this premium stuff for a prominent customer in the area, a former Texas Ranger. I'll sell you a glass, but I'm holding the rest for my customer--"

"I don't believe we've met, My name's Clay Holland, Sheriff of Bent Creek." The Sheriff's insertion into the conversation interrupted Sam's remark and cut-off an attempted reply by the stranger, whose mouth had opened and then hesitated. "I make it my business to be the welcoming committee for visitors to our fair town. And just what is your name and business here in Bent Creek?"

The stranger glared at the Sheriff, and all activity in the saloon froze as others watched to see what would unfold. There was a momentary silent standoff, and Ranger O'Toole stepped clear to give flank support to his fellow lawman. Clearly outnumbered, the stranger cracked a quick smile, limited only to his lips, a took a swig of the premium whiskey before replying.

"Name's Harlan Hawkins, sheriff. I'm looking at investing in some property hereabouts. But I must say that this sure don't feel like no welcome committee to me." The man's broad stance and icy tone of his voice sent back a challenge to the small-town sheriff.

"And what might that investment be?" Backing his colleague, Ranger O'Toole had a wide smile on his lips, a lit cigarillo in his teeth, and his right hand hovered above his Colt.

"He done called in the note to Jonsie's ranch and give him five days to get out." The emotional voice came from the card table. Ranch hand Deever, flushed and angry, was now standing. "Jonsie gave final wages and let me go yesterday."

"What gall you got calling in a note? Just who the hell are you and what you trying to pull in my town?" The Sheriff was getting heated, stepping into the man's face, spittle flying. There were some grumblings from the others in the saloon as they began to understand the impact of what was occurring.

The spiffy-looking stranger held his ground, body squared towards the Sheriff. He casually lifted the glass from the bar and sipped slowly, giving an exaggerated display of enjoying the premium whiskey. "It's just business, gentlemen. My investors and I feel there's prime opportunity to grow this little community."

Harlan Hawkins set the glass on the bar next to the gold piece he had dropped there moments before. "No change necessary. Start me a tab, and order a case of that Tennessee whiskey." He turned and walked towards the door. Over his shoulder, the drinkers heard his parting shot, "Any problems with that, I might just buy the place, get rid of the riff-raff."

"Who the hell does he think he is," grumbled the Sheriff as he took a swallow from his glass. "I'm gonna find out what he's up to. Nobody comes into my town throwing their weight around like that."

The card game no longer held an interest among the players. The men in the bar were sharing their thoughts about the uppity stranger in fancy clothes coming to town and pushing his weight around. Dealer Leverett Brockton III scooped up his earnings, assembled the deck, and then spoke loudly over the mix of conversation between the drinkers at the Cattleman's. "I know that man, he crossed me in St. Louis, got me removed from the Robert E. Lee. I'm surprised he didn't recognize me when he came in here. He's an operator, he is."

The Sheriff gestured to Sam to pour a drink for the gambler. "Here, Brockton, drink's on me. Tell me everything you know about that pompous bastard."

The gambler seemed to puff up now that he was the center of attention, standing taller, and straightening his worn tired suit. Brockton took a long slow swallow, savoring the bight and wiping his lips on his sleeve. The others gathered around, not wanting to miss a beat.

"Name's Harlan Hawkins, outta St. Louis. He's an operator, he is. First heard about him during the 1869 Black Friday gold scandal, he was one of them buying up that gold trying to get a corner of the market with them New York railroad tycoons, Jay Gould and Fisk, uhm, James Fisk was his name."

Gambler Brockton took a swallow of whiskey between each sentence and then paused to look at his empty glass. The Sheriff gestured to Sam for a refill to keep the information coming. Then the gambler continued. "Working in St. Louis, he made a ton of money in that gold market and was a big shot with the riverboats that operated up and down the ole muddy Missiipp. I was working the riverboats at that time."

"Yeh, I remember that," said the Sheriff. "President Grant ordered the sale of gold to stop the speculation."

His glass refilled again, Brockton continued his story. "Then later, he was working with some bankers, and involved in making deals and speculation in land in St. Louis, Chicago, and Memphis. Some of them deals were with that Jay Cooke and Company, pushing prices up and making him a lot of money. They say that's what caused the New York stock market to close in 1873."

"So, how does a riverboat gambler like you get involved with this spiffy big shot businessman," asked Ranger O'Toole. "And, how come you're here dealing cards to cowhands who barely make thirty a month wages instead of hitting the high rollers on the Robert E. Lee?"

"Well, some of the businessmen riding the boats were doing deals with him and they talked about those deals when playing cards. I just listened, and worked my game,"

"So they were losing their money to Harlan Hawkins at the bank and losing their shirts to you on the riverboat!" exclaimed the Ranger. Everybody roared in laughter at that remark.

Brockton smiled at the joke and then looked at his empty glass once again. By now, the Sheriff was wise to Brockton's game, he held his hand up to stop Sam from refilling the glass. "So, mister riverboat gambler, what brought you to our fine little town dealing cards to fellas making cowhand wages instead of high rollers on the Robert E. Lee?"

Brockton flushed in embarrassment that his empty glass routine had been exposed and that he now as expected to provide details of his fall from grace as a prima donna on the big stage to working the dusty floors of the Cattleman's Saloon. "Well, one of the fellers who joined my game on the Robert E. Lee lost money that was to be used in his deal with Harlan Hawkins, and Hawkins got me removed from the boat."

Chapter 13

"What proof you got that you own this property?"

Sitting in the front room of the small building that served as office and jail for the Sheriff of Bent Creek, finishing up some steak and eggs from the Red-eye Saloon, Sheriff Clay Holland and Texas Ranger O'Toole were planning a divide and conquer strategy to deal with the recent events affecting the small ranching community. The big issue was the rustling of a flock of sheep and the theft of an exceptional Arabian horse.

Ranger O'Toole had been sent to the area by the Ranger Captain in Austin because of various reports attributing thefts to a man called the ghost bandit because no one had seen this person and reports of the thefts had been popping up in various areas of west and southern parts of the state. But now they had new information. MacDonald's son, Dennis had seen and described a child who had played a deceptive role in the theft, and then Dennis had seen a rider on the valued Arabian, a man who had the appearance of a ghost. The Ranger would pursue these leads focusing primarily on tracking the valued horse. A teamster returning from a delivery to the Del Rio area had related stories from residents of that area about a reported theft by children. Today, Ranger O'Toole headed west.

Sheriff Clay Holland now had a new issue to consider with the appearance of a stranger, a spiffy dressing easterner named Harlan Hawkins who had succeeded in taking a ranch from local rancher Jones, by calling in a note from the bank that had provided some funding for purchase and operations of the small ranch. Offhand, the Sheriff was not sure whether a law had been broken. While Jones had reported a theft after seeing children in the area, he had not come to town to complain or report any theft relating to the ownership of the ranch. The matter had come out the day that the stranger had come into the Cattleman's Saloon and ranch hand Deever reported that he had been fired by Jones because of the impending loss of the ranch to the banker.

The Sheriff was going to investigate this matter further to see if any laws had been broken. But this was different than the usual law enforcement duties of a west Texas Sheriff because there had been no gunplay, no killing, no drunken brawl, and no rustling of a herd. As a man who had lived by his wits for thirty years as a Texas Ranger, and now as a small-town Sheriff, these were new challenges. He knew he needed to stay in front of this, and began by drafting a letter to Judge Hiram Jackson in San Antonio about what laws if any might be violated by Harlan Hawkins' actions. He left the letter with Merchant McCann because the east-west stagecoach route between San Antonio and Del Rio provided the post service.

As the Sheriff came out of McCann's Mercantile, he saw two teamsters' wagons sitting in the roadway near an open area across from the stable. He walked down that direction to investigate. The drivers sat quietly talking to each other, watching the man with a badge on his shirt approach.

"Howdy. You gentlemen lookin' for somebody? Or maybe some directions? I'm Sheriff Holland, maybe I can help."

"Nope. Just waiting for directions on where to drop the load."

"Well, I can give directions. Where you headed? Whose expecting this delivery?" Now the Sheriff was curious. He looked into the back of the wagons to see what was being delivered. He saw that the wagons were loaded with cut lumber and supplies, supplies used in building construction. "So where you headed? Who's getting supplies to build?"

Just then Harlan Hawkins rode up in a buggy. As before, he was spiffily dressed in a dark gray woolen suit with a white shirt, string tie, and rounded derby hat. He ignored the Sheriff and spoke directly to the teamsters. "You made good time I see. You got a bill of lading for me to see? Let's have it.

Hmmm. Ok, Ok. Good, " he said as he looked at the papers. "Just unload right there near that Oak. A crew should be here shortly."

"Hawkins!" the Sheriff barked loudly. "I won't be ignored. What the hell is going on here?"

"I'm building a bank on this land." Hawkins had a way of holding his head high and looking down his nose at others, even if they were eye to eye.

"You're what? The hell you are. This ain't your land." The Sheriff had stood up to lynch mobs in his days as a Ranger, but something about this man just seemed to prompt an intense reaction from the people he dealt with.

"It's my property. I can build what I please. And I'm building a bank here. As a sheriff, you should appreciate the benefits of a bank for a growing community."

Another wagon arrived and four men climbed down, looking like laborers from the city, certainly not giving the appearance of the typical west Texas ranch hand. One man began giving directions to the others about unloading and unrolling a large paper with sketches and dimensions.

"What proof you got that you own this property?" From a recent court case last year over a land dispute involving a homesteader and his former Ranger partner and now prominent local rancher James Smith, the Sheriff was familiar with legal documents detailing land ownership.

"Everything's in order. I'd be happy to show you if you think you'll understand these legal documents." Hawkins didn't miss an opportunity to try to belittle others to bolster his own importance.

"Lemme see. I've dealt with courts and court papers," barked the Sheriff as he rustled through the documents. "What? What the hell? Says here you bought this property from James Smith."

"So? No Texas law requires that purchase or sale of real property must be approved by the local sheriff. I have an approval for a state-chartered bank. I made an offer for the land and Smith sold the land to me and my investors. Now, if you don't mind, Sheriff, I've got a project to direct."

"I'll be damned," grumbled the Sheriff. "I'm going to have a word with Smith."

The men were pounding stakes into the ground and running strings to square off an area for the new building, as Harlan Hawkins strolled across the site, papers in hand pointing in one direction and then another as he gave instructions. Sheriff Holland returned to his office and busied himself with straightening up the place. Several old wanted posters were pulled down and others re-arranged to fill the space. He swept the pine floor and patched a small crack in the wall by the back door. The bars on the windows and the cells were solid, no maintenance was needed there. A small office with one desk and two chairs, a rack for rifles, a posting board with wanted notices and a small sleeping room by the back door turned out to be a quick clean, at least by a man's standards.

He checked the ammunition supply kept in the drawer under the rifle rack on the wall; six boxes of .44-40 for the Winchesters, better re-order. The .45 ammo for the Colt kept in the bottom desk drawer was down to three boxes; he'd re-stock a couple from McCann's and place reorders on both. It didn't seem as though he had been using as much ammo as in the old days, there were longer periods between re-orders and it didn't seem as though there was a need to keep as big of a reserve supply. When he had begun as Sheriff in Bent Creek four years ago, he had kept a large reserve supply of ammunition and had occasion to use it, but since that time, many of the bad seeds had been jailed or runoff or, in a few cases, killed because they thought they could outdraw an aging Sheriff in his fifties.

The bottom desk drawer on the right side held his bottle of whiskey and a couple of glasses. It was a natural reaction, without even thinking, and he was sipping on a half-filled glass as his mind reflected on the old days as a Ranger. He recalled the loss of wife Sarah due to the gunplay of a stage robber, one Josiah Judd, and the fortuitous events of last fall when he was able to track and kill the man who had killed his wife. He vividly pictured that day, the chase, the exchange of bullets, the man's refusal to give up, the flanking movement allowing him to close in, and the six bullets bringing justice to the killer of sweet Sarah. And yet, as the smoke had cleared and he looked down at the bleeding dead body of outlaw Judd, he remembered his words, 'it's done, Sarah.' And yet to this day an emptiness still remained.

The glass of whiskey was empty and the savory flavor called for more. A refill emptied the bottle, he would get another from Sam at the Cattleman's before the sun went down. The second glass was warming, without the bite of the first as his insides welcomed the whiskey. A mellow glow had settled over his body chasing away the anger from the confrontation with the city slicker Harlan Hawkins, who it seemed was going to be a player in Bent Creek.

But, the events of this week had a new element, the law, it seemed was speaking more through papers and the pen rather than speaking through bullets and guns. He was determined to enforce the law in Bent Creek, but it had seemed that the Jones ranch had been taken as a result of the bank papers. When Jones came to town, The Sheriff quizzed him about the events and Jones had confirmed that there was a banknote and that he had missed a payment causing the bank to demand that he pay off the loan or, failing that, to turn the ranch over to the bank's representative, who happened to be this Hawkins fellow. And now, again today here is this Hawkins fellow with a sales agreement showing he bought the property and will be building a bank in Bent Creek. To Sheriff Clay Holland, a man dedicated to enforcing the law, this just didn't feel like justice. He tipped his head back to catch the last drops of whiskey in the now empty glass.

"If there's a way to stop this guy, I'll find it," growled the Sheriff as the empty glass came down hard on the desktop.

Chapter 14

Hawkins called in the note on the ranch.

The morning began with the banging of hammers against lumber as the work crew across the street had begun at the crack of dawn. Even from the sleeping room in the back, the pounding hammers sounded like civil war cannons to a man with a whiskey-induced headache. Sheriff Holland rolled out of bed and stumbled to the desk drawer for a little hair of the dog, but found only the empty bottle, reminding him of the cause of his present condition. For some reason today, he was hungry as a horse, so he headed out the door of the tiny office straight for the Red-eye.

"Quit that damn banging," he yelled to the workers across the street. The workers stopped momentarily looking to see who called but resumed their task at the barked order of the site foreman.

The Sheriff walked into the Red-eye expecting to see the smiling face of proprietor Betsy Brown, looking for some of her special Irish coffee. Several men were huddled around a table in a corner deep in conversation. As he took a step to his usual table near the kitchen, Betsy floated out with her hands full of plates piled high with steak and eggs steaming an enticing aroma that made his stomach growl. The big-busted comely Betsy passed the Sheriff without notice or recognition, stopping at the table where the three men sat, interrupting their conversation as the hostess arrived with the food.

"Why thank you, Miss Betsy. Such service and, oh my, such a smile to top it off."

The Sheriff felt his headache intensify and his fist tighten in anger. It was that bastard Hawkins, here, and Miss Betsy flitting around like a schoolgirl on Saturday dance night. They were talking and laughing, and she was chirping like a mother robin feeding her chicks, ignoring her best and regular customer. He had a lot of nerve coming in here like that.

"I'll get it for you," chirped Betsy and she spun from the table and the three laughing men. As she glided quickly back towards the kitchen, her petticoats swishing, she nearly bumped into the Sheriff as he stood there slightly dumbfounded at her coquettish enthusiasm for this other man whom he considered a troublesome outsider that should be run out of town. "Pardon me, I'm in a hurry, he-he-he."

"A little service here if you're not too busy," growled the Sheriff as Betsy floated on tip-toes bringing coffees for the Hawkins and his two associates.

"Oh Clay, quit acting like you sat on a bumble-bee. I've been busy with an important new customer. You're not my only customer you know. Now, what do you want?" She was breathless and her face flushed with excitement.

"Well, I came in here for your special coffee and steak and eggs, but I just lost my appetite," the Sheriff grumbled as he turned and went towards the door.

"Why Clay, I do believe that you're jealous!" Betsy laughed, standing arms akimbo getting in the last word as the door banged behind the angry Sheriff.

There was laughter from inside the Cattleman's Saloon prompting the angry Sheriff to keep walking, and the pounding of hammers continued as the workers had squared off stringers and were laying a floor showing the shape of the foundation for the new building under construction. His headache pounded in rhythm with the hammers so he headed straight for the stable to get the roan. Hostler Washington was nowhere to be seen, so the Sheriff led his choice mare from the stable, tossed on a blanket, saddle, and bridle, snugged the fittings, and then gritted his teeth from the headache pain as he lumbered up to the saddle, and clicked the roan to a lope.

As a younger man, there had been many a day that he was in the saddle with no breakfast and a drink-addled headache, so why should this time be any different? But that was some thirty years ago; now in his fifties, the ole body seemed to complain about hard use with greater and longer-lasting pain than in the old days. The jostle of the ride seemed to make his stomach upset, and by the time he had turned north towards the Smith Ranch, he had to rein in the roan and lean to the side as his stomach upheaved the last remnants of yesterday's whiskey.

The ride settled into a routine, and he let the horse set its own pace. The animal seemed to sense the rider's discomfort and assumed an ambling gait with a minimum of jolting bounce and continued northward like it knew the destination to be the Smith Ranch. One hour became two, and the clear air, the solitude of the ride was soon brightened by the occasional chittering of house sparrows in areas where there were some trees, and then the killdeers presented their resounding "kill-dee, kill-dee" in the open prairies where their fiery orange rump and pointy wings were visible as they ran along the ground looking for bugs and beetles.

The sprawling Smith Ranch was its usual bustle of activity, with sounds of bawling cattle, the clump and snorts of working horses, the yelps and whistles of cowboys, and the clanging of a blacksmith working metal. An aroma of cooking steak mixed with wood smoke pleasantly filled the air as the Sheriff approached the large two-story central ranch house. The Smith's Chinese cook, Yáng Chao was turning a large carcass of beef on an outdoor fireplace with a moving spit set close to the roaring fire to sear the meat before raising it for an even cook.

"Good afternoon, Sheriff, sir," said the slim-statured man as he kept his eyes on the task at hand. "Tie up over there. Mr. Smith be back soon; he be checking on condition of a newborn calf and the mama cow."

Hunger pangs in the Sheriff's stomach responded to the smells as he tied up the roan. "Mighty fine piece of meat there, Mr. Chao, well-tended in your hand."

The cook picked up a large knife and fork, deftly slicing a piece of browned beef from a tip and handing the fork to the Sheriff to taste right from the fork.

"Afternoon Clay. Staying for dinner?" James Smith, a former partner with Clay Holland when they were Texas Rangers in their younger days, shared a bond beyond friendship from that experience. Together, they had faced hostile Indians, outlaws, and rampaging mobs, often severely out-numbered, using their wits and their courage to overcome long odds and defeat an adversary or diffuse a tense situation.

"Appreciate the offer. After the sample I've just tasted, I'd be a fool to do otherwise." There was a bit of small talk beginning with the status of the newborn calf, and then the men adjourned to Smith's ranch office for some of that Tennessee whiskey that Smith special ordered for his private stock.

They sat in a couple of horse-hide chairs in front of the large river-rock stone fireplace as flames crackled. After a glass of the premium whiskey had been shared and a second poured, the Sheriff posed the question that prompted his half-day ride out to the Smith Ranch. "There's a new feller in town, name of Hawkins, Harlan Hawkins, started building a bank on the empty lot across from the stable. Says he purchased the land from you. That true?"

"Yep."

"Then, you know this feller? You think he's somebody should be having a say in how we do things here in Bent Creek?" The Sheriff was treading carefully, knowing that since they had left the Ranger service, James Smith received a land grant for the land he now occupied and had built this fine ranch home and had expanded his holding by acquiring adjoining properties and growing his heard of long-horns to the thousands, facts that gave him a different perspective to many issues.

"A banker by reputation, he came recommended from folks in San Antonio," Smith said, going along with the Sheriff's line of questions. But the curtness of replies showed that he held his cards close, feeling that he didn't have to justify a business decision to the town sheriff, despite their former Ranger relationship.

"You never wanted no bank in town before. What's different now?"

"I'm not no banker. I'm a rancher, and need to manage my herd and my ranch." Then Smith pushed back. "Real estate deals aren't subject to a local Sheriff's jurisdiction. What's with the questions?"

"This feller Hawkins, he called in the note that Jones had on his ranch. Jones fired Deever, and he has till the end of the week to get off the land, lock stock and barrel." The Sheriff let the words sink in momentarily, waiting for a reaction. Smith sat impassively. "It ain't right, I tell ya, Jonesie took a hit from that thief Chavez. He shouldn't be forced out because of that."

"Have another drink, Clay," Smith said finally and refilled the glass in front of his former partner. "Running a ranch, a big one like this, it takes a lot, it gets complicated. I took a hit too, losing a number of head 'cause that Chavez stampeding the herd. We left a few strays down by Jones on account of he helped on that round-up. He was in arrears back then and hit me up for a loan. I had to say no. I hadn't had a drive in two years, not till this month when just made it back in that damn blizzard."

They continued the talk through dinner, joined by ramrod Buck Carroll. Smith said he'd see if he could find a spot for cowhand Deever who had lost his job. The conversation drifted about other events occurring around Bent Creek, the traveling medicine man, and the current hunt for the *Bandido Fantasma.* Up to now, Smith hadn't encountered any wayward kid or seen any evidence of thievery by this bandit.

After dinner, the Sheriff thanked his host for a fine meal and mounted the roan for the trip back to town. As he rode the return trip under the late winter darkening skies, and the whipping cold of the wind, he thought about how the relationship between himself and Smith had changed over the past four years during his tenure as Sheriff for Bent Creek. He still had the same role, the same lawman's perspective as he had when working as a ranger for forty dollars a month. Sure, he had a little bigger salary now, but Smith, as the owner of the prosperous ranch now had a totally different viewpoint. Sometimes, now finding themselves on opposite sides of an issue as had been the case when Smith ranch hand Johnny Barton had shot the sheriff, Smith had not been cooperative in the search for the fugitive, his own employee. And now, once again, this matter of banks and ranch finances seemed to be putting the old partners at odds once again.

He buttoned up his denim jacket and nudged the roan into a canter to pick up the pace. The horse welcomed the exercise and there was enough light from a first-quarter moon to light the trail. Somewhere a coyote howled, and as they passed a stand of cottonwoods trailing along a creekbed, the Sheriff caught the motion of what looked to be an owl diving through the trees after a mouse or opossum or some other critter of the night.

As horse and rider neared the turn to the roadway between Bent Creek and San Antonio, the roan's ears twisted in response to some unheard sound. The Sheriff touched his Colt for reassurance. Then he heard a rustling in the bushes back off of the trail followed by a kick and bounce of a stone onto other rocks. He jerked the reins to the right and spurred the roan to charge into the bushes directly at the sound. There was a high-pitched squeal a few feet ahead, then stumble noises and scrambling feet running through the underbrush towards some nearby trees.

The roan followed the noise and the Sheriff had a lariat circled and thrown drawing on old skills remembered from cowhand days many years before. Once the thrown lariat had circled the moving target, the loop was jerked and the roan stopped dead, causing the fleeing target to be upended, just like the standard tie-down roping contests that the cowboys held on the ranch where he had worked as a young man. The Sheriff dismounted to check his prize.

Chapter 15

"I don't know his name; they call him the Ghost Bandit."

It was late when he rode into town; his captured prize was a young boy who refused to talk but showed a determination to run at the first opportunity. There had been something gimpy about the boy's movements back in the brush but there was no obvious life-threatening injury. Because the boy had attempted to flee, he was placed in the saddle in front of the Sheriff where he could be observed and contained.

The roan was left at the stable in the caring hands of hostler Washington. The boy looked longingly as Washington offered an apple treat to the horse.

"*¿Manzana?*" Apple asked Washington. The boy swallowed and tried to twist away from the Sheriff's grasp.

Washington handed the boy a ladle of water scooped from a nearby bucket, and they watched as he guzzled the water, drips running down his chin. "I know little of the Mexican tongue, but that youngin there, he knows that *manzana* is apple and good to eat. Try Doc. He know some Mexican tongue."

The boy in hand, the Sheriff knocked on Doc's door and they were welcomed in the small front room that housed an old army cot that doubled as a seat for visitors or a bed for injured who were always welcomed and aided by the aging soldier who had rendered first aid to injured and dying comrades on civil war battlefields. The room was lit by a kerosene lamp and a book sat open pages down next to the flickering flame that gave shadows a dancing quality across the room.

"Found this youngin out in the bushes north of town. Won't speak a lick, kept trying to make a break for it till he saw the apple treat that Washington offered the roan. So thirsty he damn near took a bath in a ladle of water over at the stable," the Sheriff explained. "I never really learned the Mex talk. Hopin' you might be able to get the boy to open up."

Doc nodded and looked at the boy, and then reached out pulled him up from the cot, and turned him around revealing the limp, giving an occasional poke and prod to his arms and legs and body, then re-checking the injured foot. The boy stood tensely, his fear evident.

"*¿Habla usted inglés?*" Do you speak English? Doc said softly. The boy's eyes registered understanding, but he remained frozen. Doc continued, "*Intiendo español.*" I understand Spanish. "*¿Tienes hambre?*" Are you hungry?

The boy's eyes widened in understanding, but he steadfastly refused to talk. Doc raised a finger in a gesture of "wait a moment," and disappeared briefly to the kitchen area of his three-room frame home. He returned with a bowl of stew, a stub of bread, and a tin cup of water. The boy inched forward, his eyes wide, following Doc like a hiding jackrabbit watches a coyote.

"*¿Como se llama?*" What is your name? Doc held the food back out of reach. An instinctive swallow was causing the boy's Adam's apple to bounce. "*¡Dimelo ahora!*" Tell me now!

The young boy was salivating so much now that he swallowed again yet spittle dripped from his lips. There was a squeaky cry, then, "*Santiago, me llamo Santiago.*" Santiago, my name is Santiago."

The ice had been broken, but they still needed more. Doc's eyes met the Sheriff's who gave a subtle shake, a wordless directive to get more information before rewarding the waif with a reward of food.

"*¿Dónde vives?*" Where do you live?

"*Vivo en Piedras Negras.*" I live in Piedras Negras.

"*¿Por qué te escondías en la pradera por la noche?*" Why were you hiding on the prairie at night?

"*Esperando.*" Waiting. The words were a squeaky mix of talk and tears. The boy had leaned forward, closer to the food; the steaming aroma of the stew filled the small room.

"*Esperando a quien? ¿Para qué?*" Waiting for who? For what?" Doc held the food just out of reach. The Sheriff gave a subtle nod in concurrence. He trusted Doc's judgment in talking to the boy.

"*El jefe.*" The boss, the reply squeaked between tears.

"*¿Dónde están tus padres?*" Where are your parents?

"*Muerto.*" Dead."

"*¿Como se llama el jefe?*" What is the name of the boss?"

"*No lo sé. Lo llaman el Bandido Fantasma.*" I don't know. They call him the ghost bandit.

The Sheriff nodded in consent. Doc handed the bowl and spoon to the boy who cradled the food in one hand and scooped and slurped its contents in between shakes and sobs, not stopping until the spoon clinked on the bottom of the empty bowl and the bread was used to mop up any remnants.

Doc filled in the Sheriff about the boy's answers to his inquiries. When asked about the missing sheep, the boy admitted his role in creating a distraction and said that the jefe had taken the animals south to the river. After a few more questions, they learned that the boy had been left in a hiding place on the prairie with instructions to loot the homes and businesses in and around Bent Creek. While the Sheriff had not seen any stolen items when he captured the waif, he would check in the morning. For now, however, he decided that he needed to keep the child in a jail cell, fearing that he would run away as soon as he had a chance. Doc offered to keep the boy in his home, and the Sheriff relented only after Doc promised to cuff the boy to the bed for the night. Doc explained to the boy what was happening so that he would not be afraid.

In the morning, the Sheriff had a quick breakfast with Washington at the stable before riding out north of town to find the hideout used by the waif. Finding the exact spot in the daytime took patience, looking for evidence of the roan's hoof prints off the roadway and checking every stand of trees north of town. Patience and persistence paid off. He found evidence of a campsite, some food items, a collection of tools, and a few items of clothing.

As he packed up the items for return to Bent Creek, he thought about what the items revealed about the thief. The items were of a sort that could be snatched and run off with, easy to carry for a youngin'. They hardly looked like items of significant value. Although, the theft at McCann's store included a gun and ammunition, and the prizes from MacDonald's place included an Arabian stallion and a flock of sheep. It was certainly not like typical bandits who robbed stagecoaches of money and valuables and payroll, or when rustlers stole herds of cattle and horses. But, this ghost bandit seemed to be using kids, homeless waifs, to steal items that could be carried away at little risk. Still, crime was crime and it was his job to put an end to it.

Chapter 16

"Sheriff. There's been a robbery!"

The harsh blizzard of a few weeks back was just a distant memory. Now spring was getting closer, the days growing longer with signs of early growth appearing on the prairie. Texas redbuds were showing their small pink flowers and patches of daisies and yellow groundsel flowers seemed to promise better days ahead. But the early morning harsh banging of nails and spikes into the timbers and lumber used to construct the bank building across the street disrupted the Sheriff's sleep. The workers were now laying flooring and starting to frame walls on the second level. This would be the biggest building in Bent Creek. And there were signs of other construction activity.

As more workers were brought in to work on this large project, what had been a tent for the carpenters grew into a rooming house at the edge of town. Just a few short months ago, the Sheriff knew everyone in town and the surrounding areas. Now, there were new faces, and Harold McCann was pleased with the increase in business at his general store. He was now arranging for two deliveries a week rather than the customary bi-weekly schedule. The groups of men coming into the Cattleman's Saloon and grown, especially after a hard day's work. Gambler Leverett Brockton III was busy with card games that grew from two or four players to frequent games for six to eight with big cash pots.

It had been a week or more since the Sheriff had been into the Red- Eye. He had found excuses to avoid stopping in after that one episode where Betsy had been too busy taking care of new customer Haran Hawkins to acknowledge his presence. Maybe it was the spring flowers, or maybe he was just really hungry for Betsy's steak and eggs because on this day he found himself standing in the doorway watching a room full of people eating and two young ladies doing their best to keep up with the seating of customers and bringing their food and drinks. The place appeared to be more crowded, with added tables and chairs to accommodate more diners.

Betsy's voice could be heard from the kitchen as she was coordinating the cooking and delivery of foods to the hungry Red-eye customers. The sheriff's customary table and chair were occupied by a man and his wife and daughter.

"Well, don't just stand there looking like a lost sheep, Clay. Come in and sit a spell." The floor-length red dress and petticoats swished as Betsy walked towards Sheriff, a glowing smile and flushed skin sparkling from hard work in a fast-paced kitchen. A strand of blonde hair had escaped the bun and danced as she walked with a spring in her step. Betsy touched his arm and steered him to a small table along a wall, and signaled one of the serving girls. "Irish coffee! You're staying for breakfast aren't you Clay? And steak and eggs, rare and scrambled!"

"Looks like you're mighty busy today," observed the Sheriff as his eyes scanned the Red-eye which operated as a saloon and restaurant. Lately, the food business had grown and drinking was secondary to hungry appetites. There was no sign of Harlan Hawkins, and the Sheriff was secretly glad that the businessman had taken his business somewhere else today.

Just then a young girl, maybe ten years of age or so came to the table with a sizzling steak and eggs in one hand and a tin cup of coffee in the other.

"Thank you, Maria," said Betsy as the girl set the food and cup on the table, glanced at the Sheriff's star on his chest, and she quickly disappeared back into the kitchen. Betsy took a deep breath, relaxing for a moment, as her eyes moved around the Red-eye checking the activity.

"Who's your little helper?" asked the Sheriff.

"Maria, she's a hard worker, but very shy. She hardly says a word."

"Daughter to one of your servers? I didn't know any of your girls had family around," observed the Sheriff. "She has Mexican look about her."

"Actually, I found her scavenging food from the waste one evening, and brought her in to give her a meal. Poor thing was starving." Betsy glanced around looking for the girl.

"For a business proprietor and operator of a saloon, Miss Betsy, you have a soft heart for the children in town and those traveling across the prairie with their families," he commented, his eyes surveying her voluptuous body in its bright red dress that matched the beauty of the cardinals singing from the treetops. "But you never have talked about children of your own."

Betsy summoned one of the servers. "Gerti, where did little Maria go?"

"I ain't seen her, Miss Betsy." Gerti disappeared back to the kitchen area. In a few moments, Gerti returned, her brow etched in concern. "Miss Betsy, I looked, an' the girl's gone. And so is the piece of loin meet we was working from. And, the bartender says there's some missing bottles of Whiskey from the storeroom."

The Sheriff set down his knife and fork. "You said you found this girl scavenging food from the waste? And now stuff is missing? How long she been coming around?"

"Last three days or so, we been so busy lately, it was good to have another hand." She took a breath and sighed. "Oh Clay, you're always so suspicious. Probably she's from one of the homesteaders in the area, they have such a hard time growing crops and this is winter and all. She's just hungry. You wouldn't deny her would you?"

"Well Betsy, dear, there's a thief in the area. Just the other day we were talking to that MacDonald boy about the theft of a flock of sheep and there was a kid who created a distraction and someone knocked him on the head and took the flock and another rider took his prize Arabian. Bonner's been tracking that."

"Yeh, so…?" Betsy was unconvinced. "Not this little girl—"

"Yes. That little girl!" The Sheriff's voice now had an edge. "I caught one last night, ten maybe twelve years old, Mexican. There's a crew of 'em working for this jefe, a Mexican boss, a guy they call the ghost bandit."

Just then, there was some noise by the doorway. Merchant Harold McCann came running into the Red-eye. "Sheriff! Sheriff Holland. There's been a robbery!"

The Sheriff stood, at least he had completed half of a steak breakfast and washed it down with a cup of Irish coffee. "Harold, what happened?"

69

"A robbery! My midweek delivery from San Antonio. They were jumped out by the north crossroad. Got away with the wagon and all!" Generally a calm man, the merchant was excitable when his business was affected.

The teamster added to the story. "There was this body in the road, we stopped and saw that it was a kid, looked to be bloody. Hurt, you know? I went to check on him. Then there's a shot, and I turn around and see Herschel on the ground rolling in pain. And then, and then—" the teamster sucks in a gulp of air before continuing. "And then that kid who was laying in the road, now he's up on the seat, whipping the reigns and turning the wagon around, and there's a shot at my feet. Stopped me in my tracks, from some funny-looking cowboy by the side of the road."

"I got Hershel over to Doc's," chimed in McCann. "They walked to town and Herschel was in pretty bad shape."

A woman gasped at the story being relayed by a man bearing bloody evidence of the tale. The servers stood around and all the patrons at the Red-eye had stopped eating, listening intently to every word of the exciting story.

"The cowboy! Tell me about the cowboy." The Sheriff pressed for more details.

"Oh man, oh man," the teamster paled and his eyes widened as he recalled the events. "I,…I couldn't see his face, a ways off, hunnert feet or more, funny looking, white,…no nose, just, slits for black eyes and mouth—"

"Ieeaayyaah—" the woman screamed this time, overcome by the excitement. Betsy stepped over to her aid, trying to steady the woman who looked like she might faint.

"Let's go," said the Sheriff. "Come with me, show me the spot. We'll track them down." The Sheriff and the teamster hurried out the door.

Chapter 17

"Look here. That there's Herschel's blood."

At the stable, ever alert to the comings and goings about town, and knowing Sheriff Holland, Washington had the roan and another horse saddled and ready to go. In minutes, the two men were riding east towards the north-south road that headed to the ranches north of town and down ultimately towards Rio Bravo and Mexico. When they arrived at the crossroads, the teamster, a chunky fellow in his fifties called John, started describing the events once again, gesturing here and there to emphasize a point or show a location.

"Kid was laying in the road here, and Herschel had stopped the team there, see here where the wheels marks show that the kid turned the wagon. And here, look here, that there's Herschel's blood where he fell when they shot him."

"And where was that cowboy, the one that shot Herschel?" asked the Sheriff.

"Over there, off the road, about a hunnert feet."

"Did he shoot Herschel with a pistol or rifle?"

"I saw a rifle in his hand, looked to be a Winchester."

"Over about here?" The Sheriff had dismounted and walked around looking for evidence of a shell casing ejected from the rifle. After a moment, he stooped to pick up something. Then he circled the ground looking at the tracks. There were tracks that looked to be those of the Arabian. He'd check this with Texas Ranger Bonner who had been tracking the outlaw. It occurred to the Sheriff, that if the outlaw had been here, on the Arabian, Bonner must have lost the trail.

"What kind of horse was the cowboy riding?"

"Oh man, ya know, as I think about it, he was on a mighty fine animal, looked like a show horse."

"What did he look like? Coloring?"

The teamster thought a moment, then replied. "Yep, mighty fine animal. It was black, a shiny black with white star forehead and four white stockings."

"That's the one we're looking for. You keep to the road, follow the wagon tracks, and take it slow. If you see anybody, lay back, and wait for me. I'm going to see where this Arabian went to. Maybe the trails join."

The Sheriff followed the trail about a quarter-mile before the tracks went through a creek bed and into the water and there was no close-by evidence of the Arabian coming out of the water up or downstream for a couple hundred yards either way. It seemed as though the intent had been to lead him away from the wagon trail. The sheriff returned to the roadway to find teamster John. In about twenty minutes, he had caught the teamster.

"Any sign of the wagon?"

"No, nothing yet."

"Any evidence that the wagon was driven off the roadway?"

"No, I was watching for that too." The teamster seemed to have it together.

After a while they came to a ridge, that looked down over a long low hollow then another ridge. The riders paused for a moment, a drink, and offered some water from the Sheriff's hat for the horses. The sun was beginning to lower on the western horizon.

"There. Look there, just over that second ridge, maybe a quarter mile up." The Sheriff squinted and pointed. "There! A dark spec moved and bobbed, it looks bigger than just a man and horse, has to be the wagon." The Sheriff nudged the roan to a canter and John followed on his mount.

In about fifteen minutes they had nearly caught the wagon. The Sheriff led his companion off the roadway to a nearby rise with a view of the road. Here, they dismounted and walked to the high point and stood near a couple of live oaks so that their profile did not show on the hill. Watching, the wagon moved steadily at a walking pace, that did not wear out the two-horse team. There was no companion rider, the cowboy did not appear to be present. Overhead a turkey vulture soared in the breezes, drifting towards the west, and the Sheriff did not catch any movement of horse or rider from surrounding areas.

"Let's get him," the Sheriff directed as they remounted and started off the ridge. "See that curve in the road, we'll circle and catch him there." They kicked the horses up to a gallop, staying wide from the road, and after a few minutes, had arrived at the curve where the road by-passed a large rocky outcropping and a few scattered boulders that nature had tumbled from the limestone formation.

"John, do you know any Mexican talk?" asked the Sheriff.

"Nope, afraid not," John replied.

"What's your command to stop the horses?"

"Whoa, and pulling back on the reins"

"Well, that kid driving the wagon looks like he's Mexican and he may not understand English. When they come around the corner, I'll block the road and say stop, you give your command to the animals." Then at the Sheriff's direction, they set up on each side of the road, with the stone formation covering their presence until the wagon rounded the last hook of the bend. Soon the creaks and rattles of the wagon could be heard. When the wagon appeared, the Sheriff put the roan in the middle of the road and called out "Stop."

"Whoa boy," called John to the team that he usually worked with. The animals listened, and the boy, sat there surprised to see the two gringos suddenly blocking his way. He shook the reins but the animals hesitated.

The young Mexican boy, seeing that the animals would not move, bolted from the wagon running towards a stand of trees. The Sheriff clicked his tongue, nudged roan, and pulled the reins in the direction of the running boy. The animal responded, and he pulled the lariat off its loop, and in about 4 steps, the boy had been lassoed and pulled to a stop just like the standard tie-down roping exercise used to catch the other boy.

"All right, amigo, you're sitting here," the Sheriff said as he pulled the young lad up to the saddle.

But this boy was bigger than the other one he had brought back to Bent Creek riding two in the saddle. Though skinny in stature, this boy stood nearly as tall as a man, probably fourteen or fifteen years old. They decided to put the boy on the wagon, next to John but tied so that he couldn't escape or cause other harm. The second horse was tethered to the wagon and John took the reins of his old team. They turned the wagon and headed north back to Bent Creek. It would be well after dark by the time they reached town.

Chapter 18

...movement...a silky white face...slits for eyes and mouth...

It was nearing midnight and a chilly late winter breeze caused uncontrolled shivers to man and beast alike as they neared the San Antonio roadway. Bent Creek was just a couple of miles more. A quarter moon peeked momentarily through breaks in unseen clouds and then disappeared again. The wagon wheels squeaked and the box rattled as the iron-coated wheels bounced over the rough trail. The animals moved at a steady walking pace in the darkness of night, the rocking and rolling of the movement causing the exhausted riders to give in to moments of dozing relief. Somewhere a coyote howled, and then a horse snorted.

The roan's ears twisted, and the mare took a hard sniff, giving a head shake that woke the Sheriff from a momentary doze. He patted the animal's neck and whispered, "What is it? What's out there?"

Up ahead, a darkness loomed, appearing to be a stand of trees. There was a sound of a hoot owl; its call sequence of rhythmic hoots—"Who's awake? me, too." The Sheriff sat up, and touched his Colt for reassurance, as his eyes scanned the darkness trying to sort to the sounds of the night, his senses now alert, checking for possible threats. There was a chill at the back of his neck, was it the cold breeze, or an instinctive alert of danger?

From the front right, there was a rustle of movement, and a simultaneous flash and bang of a gunshot, a scream of pain, and John fell backward into the wagon bed. In the flash, there was a momentary image, an image of a horse and rider, and a growled command. *"¡Joven, toma las riendas!"* Young one, take the reins!

Actions seemed to occur in slow motion in front of the Sheriff, the shot, thud of a bullet finding its mark, a cry of pain, and a man falling backward from the seat of the wagon. There was a movement from the side, a rider, a man with sombrero style hat, a silky white face that shimmered, showing slits of two eyes and a mouth, and a silver Colt coming to bear as hooves stomped the ground, a shiny black horse with white star face.

The Sheriff rolled to his left, Indian style, hanging on to the saddle horn, taking cover behind the body of the roan as this ghost of a man and horse attacked. The roan lurched to avoid the charging animal, and a gunshot blazed nicking the Sheriff's right shoulder as the animal's paths crossed. The wagon had lurched forward, the young Mexican boy somehow managing to grasp the reins and attempting to steer the team to circle back towards the south. His shoulder cringing in pain, but hanging on to the saddle, the Sheriff managed to lead the roan alongside the excited team. He pulled himself back into the saddle and reached for the bridle and reins of the closest team horse, calling out a whoa, and pulling back to slow the wagon.

Now off the road in a dry wash, the wagon slowed. From up by the roadway, the Sheriff heard a shot and felt the whistle of a bullet as his hat flew off. He drew his colt and returned fire, in the direction of the bang, hearing a grunt and then the sound of galloping hooves in the darkness. He thumbed a second shot in the direction of the fleeing animal, but aimed high, to avoid injuring the prize animal.

"What happened?" It was teamster John, crawling from the boxes of goods in the wagon back to the driver's seat. "Oh, my arm. Who shot me?"

"Some bandido tried to hijack the wagon. I scared him off. Nicked me too. Let's get back to town." There was tightness in the Sheriff's voice as he continued to pull the bridle of the lead horse back to the roadway.

As they neared Bent Creek, there was a whistle from the darkness, causing the roan to shake its head and snort in recognition. "This is Sheriff Holland, who goes there?"

76

"Yessa Sheriff, this here's Washington." There was a movement from a copse of trees along the road and then the glistening of a rifle barrel. "I heard shots in the distance, come out to check."

"Comin' back with the hijacked wagon. Had to fight for it," replied the Sheriff. "Keep an eye out, he may still be around."

Because the youth had tried several times to escape and had been caught with the stolen wagon, the Sheriff left his prisoner locked in the jail for the time being. They parked the wagon in front of McCann's store and rousted him to accept its contents, before heading over to Doc's to care for the bullet wounds.

Doc assessed his two patients and decided to start on John first because his injury was more serious and required the removal of a bullet. As Doc began working on John, the young Santiago walked in from the backroom to watch.

"What's this one doing waking around loose? You agreed to keep him tied up if he were gonna stay here rather than behind bars over at my place. The Sheriff's voice was sharp, still excited from the gunplay earlier in the evening.

"He's all right. We reached an agreement. He behaves, he got free roam of the place." Doc spoke over his shoulder while keeping his eyes on the bleeding bullet hole in John's arm. He splashed some whiskey on the would causing John to grimace. Doc handed the bottle to John, saying, "Drink this, just a couple of swallows." Then glancing over his shoulder to first to the boy and then to the Sheriff, "Any stunts, he'll learn how I take out fingernails."

In the morning, the Sheriff rolled out of bed slowly, aching all over, and the pain strongest in his right bi-cep where that bullet had winged him the night before. The bandages were still tight and only showing just a little bleeding overnight. Outside the banging of hammers continued as the bank construction continued. His free left hand searched the floor under his cot and found the whiskey bottle where it had been left the night before. The first swallow burned but the second emptied the contents and helped to get the aging lawman's body back on track. The young Mexican prisoner was sprawled on his back, one arm across his eyes; a slow breath followed by a growling snore giving evidence of heavy sleep after a night-time adventure.

The whack of the hammers to nails was muffled only slightly as the sounds now echoed from behind a front wall of what was now a two-story building. The sheriff made quick stops at the Cattleman's Saloon, and then at Doc's before crossing the street to the Red-eye Saloon. His eyes scanned the patrons, noted the absence of the banker Harlan Hawkins, and found the open table along the wall where Betsy had fed him steak yesterday. Betsy came swishing from the kitchen in her brilliant red dress, smiling upon seeing the Sheriff; then her expressions switched to an etch of concern as she saw the bandage on his shoulder.

"Now what did you do, Clay!?"

"Just a nick. I've had horses kick me harder," he minimized the toll that the job took on his body. One of the servers handed him a steaming cup that gave an aroma of coffee with a hint of the whiskey that was "the usual" morning beverage he received at the Red-eye. He nodded "yes" when Betsy silently mouthed the words "steak and eggs?" They sat and surveyed the busy room, sipping their coffees before speaking again.

"That girl, the little Mexican..." he hesitated, trying to recall her name.

"Maria? Yes, what about her?"

"Yesterday she turned up missing, and some food and whiskey, did she return? Show up today?"

Betsy's eyes scanned the room again before answering. "No, no she did not. I haven't seen her, nor have the other girls."

A server brought a sizzling steak and eggs, and the Sheriff cut a slice of the meat and watched the juices flow onto the plate. He took a bite and washed it down with coffee. "Anything else missing?"

"No, not that I know of,....Now, Clay, she's just a little girl, I'd be happy to give her food every day, no questions asked. I don't want you chasing that little girl across the desert like she's a horse thief."

The Sheriff had a mouthful and was working his teeth to be able to speak again, but it had been a big bite. Betsy continued talking.

"I already heard this morning that you put another child in that jail of yours last night. Clay! How can you?" Her beautiful blue eyes bore into his with a disapproving scowl.

He took another gulp of coffee and dabbed his wet lips with a napkin, trying his best to not let Betsy's feminine wiles and excellent cooking diminish his law enforcement authority.

"That youngin' was part of an attack and theft of a freight wagon resulting in bullet wounds to two teamsters and myself."

Betsy's eyes widened in surprise. "A boy, No! They're children. How can you?"

"A thief is a thief and a rustler is a rustler, regardless of age. They're not innocent children. They're part of a, …a gang of thieves. They steal animals, guns, tools, food, and alcohol. If that girl was so innocent, why did she steal your whiskey after you gave her food?"

Betsy persisted. "But, Clay, they're just children, you can't ---"

"Now Betsy, if you had children, you wouldn't let them get away with that," the Sheriff's voice rose in anger. "If you had children, you'd stop them. You would punish them. Tell me you wouldn't."

Betsy's eyes grew like saucers and her face flushed. She had never heard Clay Holland, the sheriff ever raise his voice like that, not to a lady, not to her. Her hand came up to her mouth as if holding in any other words that might erupt. She swallowed, and words escaped. "But, …but they're children."

"Spare the rod and spoil the child!" It came out calm and hard. "It may be heavy-handed, but it's justice." The Sheriff stood, dropped a gold coin on the table, and turned and walked to the door. He stopped and turned. Miss Betsy, if you please, I will be needed three squares for my prisoner. Thank you."

Chapter 19

"...ain't no ghost. Blood trails south."

After the heated discussion with Betsy Brown, the Sheriff stormed down the main street of Bent Creek, passing several townspeople without notice, his mind still racing about the fact that Betsy would question his judgment, question his authority. Throughout his twenty-some years as a Ranger and now as a town sheriff, he had dealt with young toughs and drunks and rustlers, and nearly everyone had stood up to him and had challenged his authority as a lawman. In those instances, he thought nothing of those actions, confronting bad people had always been part of the job. There was a bit of a rush, an excitement in taking on bigger men, larger numbers of men, even mobs, and coming out ahead by using your wits, your fists, or your guns to put down the troublesome situation. Every Ranger and every sheriff had such a story to tell, usually more than one.

But today, today was different. In that ten minutes, talking to that woman, that woman with the warm smile, soft blue eyes, that woman with the creamy complexion under blonde hair that escaped her control giving an unspoken sense of wildness challenging control, that woman with the buxom bosom, and swishing robust red dress that gave a man a hesitation, a hesitation that made a man stop and think, a hesitation that even the fiercest enemy combatant could not achieve.

It was not even nine in the morning when a large shit-house of a man, over 250 solid pounds, stumbled out of the Cattleman's drunk as a skunk, tripping off the planked walkway, onto the dusty street between the rows of buildings that made up the main street of Bent Creek, and slamming into Sheriff Holland.

"Hoof," mumbled the drunk as the two bodies made contact. The Sheriff, angry and confused reacted to the seething emotions stirring within. He stepped aside with the flow of impact and his arms grabbed the clumsy lout and flung him in the direction of fall, sending the drunk tumbling face-first into a mud puddle of horse urine.

The Sheriff found himself at the stable, looking in an empty stall for the roan. Still stewing, and now upset that the roan was not where expected, he reached up to pull the saddle that was hanging over the stall wall, planning to find another animal in the back lot. But as he hoisted the saddle there was resistance and he could not pull the saddle clear of the stall.

"Sumbitch," growled the man with a fury of pent-up anger as he gave the saddle another body-heaving yank, causing the hung-up cinch buckle to pull the top two boards off the stall wall.

"Mista Sheriff suh, doan you go breaking down my stable suh!" Washington's voice came from the back of the stable carrying the authority of a corporal leading a cavalry charge.

"Oh shit." The Sheriff stood stunned, suddenly aware of what he had done. "I need to go for a ride. I'll,…I'll fix it when I get back."

Washington took the saddle to the back of the stable where he had been checking the roan, and got the blanket and saddle and bridle on and adjusted. The Sheriff swung up into the saddle and lit a shuck, kicking the roan into a gallop from inside the stable and out the big door.

"Must be woman trouble to do that to a man as calm as the Sheriff. Oh my!" Washington shook his head as he pulled the large barn door closed.

The Sheriff pushed the roan pretty hard for about fifteen minutes. By that time, he was out near where he had encountered the horseman with the sombrero and the strange-looking shiny white face. He slowed the roan to a walk, giving it a rest as he looked at the area trying to recall where the gunfire had occurred. The roan's ears twitched and the animal snorted. Then a voice called out.

"Hey Clay, you trackin' the Arabian?" It was Texas Ranger Bonner O'Toole. "He led me here."

"Well, as a matter of fact, I am. I had a run-in with some feller last night, and he looked to be riding a black horse with a white star face and sheen to the hide. We exchanged some shots, but I couldn't see where he went."

"Well he come up this way, from the south, I saw tracks showing some action with a wagon. Then it looks like he was up here waiting a bit and I seen some action with prob'ly the same wagon. That you with the wagon? Now that I see your animal, and her mark, I seen some of your roan tracks around that wagon."

"Yes, it was me. He had stolen the supply wagon delivering to McCann's place. Shot up one man. I was heading out with the second teamster," the Sheriff explained. "We caught the wagon and was bringing it back when somebody bushwhacked us. Musta been him."

"Well you musta got a piece of him, there's blood over here." Bonner lit a black cigarillo, his favorite smoke.

"Good to know there's blood. From the looks of him, I thought he might a damn ghost. Has a strange, uh, spooky shiny white face, I don't mean this," the Sheriff said pointing to the pale color of his open palm, "but white like a piece of paper, shiny like the midnight moon, slits fer eyes and mouth, but don't really look like no human face."

"No wonder, they call this guy the ghost bandit," said Bonner with a smirk and a twinkle in his eye. "Blood on the ground means he's a living breathing human. Ain't no damn ghost. Let's get this guy, blood trails south."

The lawmen shared a chuckle and rode south for about an hour and lost the trail in a creek, searched for nearly another hour before giving up and heading back north towards town.

Chapter 20

"That money stays here. Or you die here."

The ride back towards town allowed the two lawmen to swap tales about Rangering experiences. Clay Holland told of cases from the old days, many including stories where he had partnered with James Smith. The animals walked at a leisurely pace as the men lit cigarillos which were a favored smoke of Bonner.

"James and I were part of the Pease River raid of 1860, going after Chief Peta Nocona when he led the push against white expansion in the northwest areas. Ya know, it's been years since I told this story," the Sheriff said as he re-lit his cigarillo, blew a cloud of gray smoke, and continued. "The chief got away, but we found that blue-eyed white woman, Cynthia Ann Parker, who had been captured by the Comanches years before."

"Yeh, I heard them stories," replied Bonner. The brass in Austin said that she insisted that she was Comanche and wanted to be returned to her people."

"They say that she's the mother of Chief Quanah, the boy warrior who became chief of the renegades who refuse to settle on the reservation." As they reached the top of a rise in the road, looking down a long decline, the Sheriff suddenly held up a hand to signal a stop to his riding companion.

"Afternoon stage stopped. Wonder what's going on," commented Bonner.

From where they had stopped, the stage and the east-west San Antonio roadway were about a half-mile ahead. The lawman could make out the stage and the horses seemed just about ant-sized, but it was hard to see any people. There seemed to be a flurry of undistinguished movement about the stagecoach, and then a horse raced away, leaving a fuzzy dust trail. About three seconds later, they heard the distant pops of gunfire. Without speaking, the two lawmen spurred their horses to an immediate gallop down the hill to the stage that remained still.

As the lawman approached, they saw the stage driver laying near the front wheel, bleeding, a woman kneeling nearby trying to tend to his injuries.

"Help up please!" called the woman, her hands bloodied apparently from caring for the injured stage driver.

"We've been robbed," exclaimed a city slicker in a dark wool business suit, stepping from behind the stagecoach. "Stole my payroll. He went that-a-way. I want you to get him."

The Sheriff recognized the businessman immediately, it was Harlan Hawkins. Anger flushed immediately. This was the man who was building the bank, the man who, in the Sheriff's mind, had stolen the Jones ranch and caused the firing of cowhand Deever, and the man who had been soliciting the attention of Betsy Brown at the Red-eye Saloon. The Sheriff turned his back on the city slicker and crouched to check on the wounded stage driver. It was a check wound, and the man needed medical care as soon as possible. Bonner was getting the story from businessman Hawkins.

"Here, use this bandana, plug that wound. Let's get him on the stage, and you get him into Doc at Bent Creek, just a few miles up the road." The Sheriff was giving directions, then turning to Hawkins. "You get up there and make yourself useful, take the reins, and bring this coach to town. What kind of horse was the robber riding?"

"A black horse, fine-looking animal," said the lady. "He, ...he had a ghostly looking face."

"What do you mean?" asked the Sheriff, as he hoisted the driver into the back of the stagecoach.

The lady looked frightened, holding her hand to her mouth. "He, his face was pale white, like a ghost, but there were no facial features, no nose, no mouth."

"Did he talk?"

"He said money. He talked like the Mexicans talk," said the lady as she climbed into the coach nest to the injured man. "What happened to the little girl?"

"Yes, that's... why I stopped," said Ben, the driver, a grimace of pain carried in his tone.

"I don't see any little girl," said Bonner, as he did a quick walk around the area. "We'll check."

The little girl had disappeared, but the trail of the Arabian horse was evident, deep tracks spread in a gallop. The stagecoach headed into town as the two lawmen followed the trail of the ghost bandit. There had been about a fifteen-minute delay from when the robbery occurred and the lawmen were on the robber's trail.

Within a mile, the trail had turned to the south, cutting across open land, a mix of bunch grasses, wildflowers, and bushes broken by occasional trees. After a while, they came to the low ridge that was an extension from the rise where they had witnessed the stage robbery some thirty minutes ago. From the ridge, in the distance ahead, there was a movement of a horse and rider.

"It's slowed, not keeping at a gallop," said Bonner as he looked through a small telescope. "But now he's headed west."

"The horse we been tracking is that Arabian, stolen from sheep farmer MacDonald up north of town. I hear tell that they're strong as a cowboys' quarter horse, good for the long haul, said the Sheriff. "If he keeps on that track, he'll by-pass Bent Creek and end up near Del Rio to cross the river."

"I know that area," said Bonner. "I was tracking him over that way last week. And as we're trailing him here, he looks to be avoiding the San Antonio – Del Rio trail. We're looking at about a two or three-day ride."

At dusk, the lawmen rested the animals near a stream. Even though there was nearly a full moon, they elected to camp and allow the animals to rest. The Sheriff found and shot a jackrabbit for a bit of meat, and Bonner had some food-stuffs in his saddlebag because he had been working the trails. The horses were able to crop some of the grasses. Both men and their animals were able to recharge.

The lawmen were up at the crack of dawn, having a quick cup of coffee and some dried beef. The lawmen talked about where they would head if they were the bandit.

"As the bird flies, I'd go straight for the river, south or southwest," said the Sheriff.

"Well, when I was hunting him over Del Rio way, there was talk that he had a hideout in the canyons and caves upriver. I'm guessing he'd head over that way," said Bonner.

As they broke up the fire and stamped out the embers, the Sheriff told his riding partner, "Bonner, I found a westward track, just like you said. I'm gonna parallel you on the roadway, try to beat him to Del Rio."

Bonner nodded, and they headed westerly, with the Sheriff going up to the main trail towards Del Rio. It was late in the day when the Sheriff had arrived in Del Rio and talked to some locals who directed him towards San Pedro Canyon just west of town. He approached the ridge that overlooked the canyon and its feeder flow towards Rio Bravo.

A little way to the south was the trail that led into the canyon. His mind flashed back to the chase a year ago with friend and former Ranger James Smith teaming up to capture the outlaw Manuel Chavez who had rustled Smith's cattle and driven them to the border. His mind flashed back to that day, his position in a stand of trees, waiting, seeing herd at the top of the hill and feeling the ground shake as they approached, watching a lead rider and aiming his Winchester to shoot the leader, with the crafty outlaw Chavez appearing behind his position with a gun aimed at his back. He is excitement rose as he recalled the thundering hooves, and his shot to fell the leader and rolling away to turn and shoot Chavez. The old Ranger partners had managed to knock off the two outlaws and turn the herd.

He rode down into the canyon, looking for a possible hide-out, a cave, or shelter. From the left side, in a nearby live oak, a crow cawed, causing the roan to snort in reply. Past the tree, in the distance, there was movement, a black horse, and a rider in a broad-brimmed sombrero approaching from another draw down to the river. The Sheriff nudged the roan down the hill stopping at a stand of cottonwoods. He tied the roan and took up a position with an open view to anyone passing into the canyon.

The black Arabian held its head high, arched tail and floating trot, like marching in a parade as it came down the hill. Little puffs of dust rose with each step. The rider with the big sombrero had his eyes on the river, hugging a satchel in his lap with one hand, and the other hand on the reins.

The Sheriff raised the Winchester sighting the outlaw on the barrel site and cocking the weapon, as he considered his shot. If he missed, the outlaw had a quick run to the river and across. From where he stood under cover of a stand of cottonwoods, he was about twenty steps to confront and block the rider. In an instant, he realized his feet were placing him in the direct path to block the outlaw in the sombrero.

"Stop right there!" The words were supported by the barrel of the 44-40 Winchester which, from the front, looks like a cannon. The animal stopped, apparently of its own accord. The man on the horse did indeed have the face of a ghost, a shiny white appearance, with no facial features, save slits for two eyes and a mouth. The Sheriff's heartbeat thumped as his mind registered this image. He inhaled deeply and breathed out slowly to calm his nerves.

"The horse stays here. That money stays here. Or you die here." The Sheriff's voice sounded loud and sure, the Winchester sighted on the man's chest.

"*Morí hace un año.*" I died one year ago, said the man with the ghost face. He drew his pistol and kicked the Arabian which responded to his command to charge the Sheriff.

BAM. The Winchester kicked in the Sheriff's arms, and a red blotch exploded on the chest of the white-faced man, causing him to fall backward to the ground. The satchel fell nearby and the round sombrero had rolled off the man's head.

The Arabian lurched forward, but the Sheriff stepped to the side. He remained focused on the target, walking up to the man who now lay on the ground, eyes flickering skyward, as a pink froth bubbled from his mouth. The Sheriff reached down and pulled off what now was obviously a white silk mask with slits for eyes and mouth, revealing a scarred and misshaped face so ugly that it took his breath away.

The Sheriff took another calming breath and looked down at the brown eyes on the scarred face. "You ain't no damn ghost. What is your name?"

The mortally wounded man looked up at the Sheriff, struggling with hard gurgling breaths. Now, Ranger Bonner O'Toole stood behind the Sheriff holding the reins of the Arabian. "*¿Como se llama?*"

"*Me llaman el Bandido Fantasma.*" They call me the Ghost Bandit. There was a gurgle from the pink froth.

"We got him," said Ranger O'Toole. He knelt down and asked the dying man another question, and the dying man spoke briefly. Then, his eyes became glassy and frozen.

"Says he's the Ghost Bandit, he helped the children nobody wanted," uttered Ranger O'Toole. Says he was the leader of the stampede of cattle from the Smith ranch, he was trampled by the cattle, making his face ugly. Says a priest gave him a mask cut from the alb, the white coat that the priests wear, so that he would not scare the children. Because it was white, the people of the village called him a ghost."

Chapter 21

"There's gonna be some heavy-handed justice around here."

The trail from Del Rio to Bent Creek was a mix of brilliant colors as south Texas emerged from a harsh winter plagued with cold temperatures and a period of knee-deep snow. There were patches of Bluebonnets sometimes spreading to cover entire fields and hills warmed by the spring sun. The brilliant blues were offset by batches of yellow and scarlet bloom called Indian paintbrush. An overnight rain had prodded the prickly pear to produce yellow and reddish floral arrays, while little bunches of hedgehog and beehive cactus sported brilliant pink blooms. Tiny brown wrens flitted about chirping with their sharp-pointed beaks foraging for insects, while yellow-bellied meadowlarks whistled from bushes along the trail.

It was late in the day, with the setting sun warming their backs as Ranger Bonner and the Sheriff rode into Bent Creek, leading the brilliant black Arabian which seemed to strut even higher in the familiar surroundings. A few people stopped and watched as the lawmen rode through the two-block-long main street. The new bank building looked nearly finished as it stood proudly guarding the prairie town's eastern entryway.

Washington emerged from the stable as if on signal as the riders approached and wearily dismounted after the two-day ride back from Del Rio.

"Welcome home, Mista Sheriff, suh, Mista Ranger O'Toole, suh." He took the reins of the three horses and led them back into the stable talking to the animals. "Looks like youse had quite a workout. Must be tired and thirsty. Ole Washington'll take care of you."

"Did you get it? Did you get my payroll?" In his easterner's wool suit and white shirt with string tie, banker Harlan Hawkins was upon the tired lawman before they could turn around.

The Sheriff, turned slowly, casually assembling the makings of a cigarette, and striking a match from his jeans. He cupped his hands, sucked the cigarette to life, and held the flame for Bonner who had a cigarillo in hand. A cloud of gray smoke hung in the air, as the lawmen's eyes met, and then they turned and walked towards the sheriff's office next door. A saddlebag hung over his shoulder.

Inside the small office, the tired lawman sat on the two chairs and the Sheriff pulled open the bottom desk drawer and pulled out his bottle of whiskey and two glasses. He poured drinks and clinked his glass with Bonner, taking a gulp and exhaling to let the fiery liquid settle in his throat. The young man, Tomas sat quietly in his jail cell, listening to the conversation in the front room.

"Well? Did you get my payroll?" Hawkins' angry voice demanded recognition.

"I have evidence from a crime in which a man was shot. I need to check on the well-being of that man. Do you have another crime to report?"

The man bristled, unaccustomed to getting push-back, his face reddening in anger. "Yes! I had a payroll stolen, I told you that on the roadway when it happened."

"How much money? And, was it cash from your pocket, or in some kind of container?"

Bonner smiled, puffing a cloud of smoke, watching the elder sheriff deal with a complaining citizen behaving like an entitled spoiled brat.

"Five thousand dollars, cash money, in tens and twenties." The man's voice was higher pitched now, almost begging.

"First of all, I'm gonna finish this whisky, check on an injured stage driver, and two injured teamsters, and have some dinner. Then, I'll check the evidence we recovered, and let you know." The Sheriff put the saddlebag in a small safe under the desk and walked out of the office and down the street.

Stopping at Doc's place, the Sheriff and Bonner found teamster Herschel up and around slowly recovering from his wound. Stage driver Ben was alive, but barely hanging on by a thread. Doc had been able to remove the bullet, but the man had received a serious chest injury and was in and out of consciousness, seemingly fighting demons in his deliriousness. Young Santiago had been a tremendous assistance in helping with the two injured men who were treated by Doc as his front room served as a make-shift hospital for the small south Texas town.

"Well look at you, Clay. You're a sight for sore eyes." Red-eye proprietor Betsy's eyes lit up in a broad smile as the Sheriff and Bonner came in for dinner.

"Good to be back, Miss Betsy." The Sheriff noticed as banker Harlan Hawkins guiltily slinked around the room and out the door after the lawmen entered. "What's cooking?"

"We've got some pot roast beef stew, with potatoes and carrots that were in the last shipment from New Orleans. It's the wonders of canning, you know."

"I'm ready. Let's eat," Bonner chimed in.

In a matter of minutes, two brimming bowl of steaming beef stew was placed before the two lawmen. Betsy had signaled for their drinks, which were brought out by little Maria. The little girl, seeing that she was bringing drinks for men wearing the brass on their chests set the drinks and quickly disappeared into the back.

"So, your little helper reappeared," asked the Sheriff.

"Now don't you get angry, Clay," Betsy admonished. "I found her out back the morning after the stage robbery, cold and starving."

"It's because she was abandoned by her jefe, the man we were chasing," said Bonner as he took a breath and filled his mouth with a chunk of beef.

"Your little girl participated in that stage robbery," the Sheriff added. "We were chasing and caught the man that preyed on little orphans to steal for him. He's dead now, admitting his actions in a dying declaration."

"Sheriff Holland, I heard you were back." Harold McCann came bustling into the Red-eye, carrying two envelopes. He handed one to the Sheriff and the other to Bonner. "Your mail came in on the stage that was robbed. I hear you brought back the stallion and the stolen payroll."

"Word travels fast," the sheriff observed. The lawmen's eyes met and they both ripped open their envelopes, and the room quieted for a moment while the letters were read silently by each recipient. "Humph, apparently our Mister Hawkins is on the up and up. Judge Jackson says that the recent business transactions are legal and instructs me to step in only if the man breaks the law. Regarding orphan children, he encourages local families to adopt them, otherwise, there's an orphanage in Houston."

"Well, little Maria can stay with me!" proclaimed Betsy. "Maria, come here, sweetie."

"An that Santiago fella, he's doing just fine with Doc," added Harold McCann.

"And about that youngin' you got in jail," said Betsy, her eyes boring into the Sheriff's eyes, "Tomas, right? Well him and Washington been striking up a friendship these last few days, the boy's learning some English, too. I think Washington might consider an extra hand at the stable."

"There's gonna be some heavy-handed justice around here," said the Sheriff. "These children gotta learn that crime don't pay, that their thieving ways are gonna stop, and that they gotta pay back what they stole."

"Well, this here letter was from the Captain of the Rangers," said Bonner. "Captain says soon as I get the Ghost Bandit case solved, I'm due back in Austin for my orders for the next assignment. I appreciate your help on this one, Clay."

"So, when MacDonald picks up his Arabian, and that banker gets his satchel of money, this case is wrapped up." The Sheriff sat back, looking at his clean plate, and empty glass of whiskey.

"Miss Betsy, introduce me to your new little helper, I need a refill here."

###

Lawman's Justice

By William S. Hubbartt

Chapter 1

Men were moving...suddenly there was gunfire.

It began like any other summer day in the Texas hill country with the calm of rich fluty whistles from yellow-breasted Meadowlarks and the repetitive warbles of rusty red Carolina Wrens at sun-up, interrupted only by the crowing of a rooster, and the baying of a mule. The brassy sun hung over the eastern horizon of Bent Creek, promising another sweltering day of suffering for man and beast alike.

Those few that moved about did so slowly, save for the fluttering of a paper fan, as a lady tried in vain to cool herself while she supervised the loading of a wagon in front of the McCann's Mercantile. Proprietor Harold McCann stood by sweating and sucking air upon finishing the job of loading the supplies into the wagon. Breathless, he had offered only a nod that the job was done, as the lady shook the reins and clucked to the horses urging the start of their journey along the dusty road towards a ranch five miles from town.

Sheriff Clay Holland, coming out of the Red-eye Saloon, tipped his hat to the lady and gave a knowing nod to Harold McCann. "Mornin', Harold."

"G' morning, Sheriff." McCann breathed heavily. The proprietor glanced up at the bright sun, squinting, hand in the air to shield his eyes. "Looks like another hot one, eh?"

"The smart folks 'll stay inside. Should be quiet and peaceful today," the aging sheriff and former Texas Ranger replied. The hard life on the Texas plains kept a man trim and in shape, but the aches and pains of aging had begun to take their toll. He did his best to hide the limp from an injured hip earned in a fall from a horse years ago.

"I hear that we're getting a new teacher. She should be arriving this week." As a general store proprietor, Harold McCann overheard the talk of townspeople and travelers alike, passing information along to the sheriff as part of their daily conversations. When an occasional newspaper arrived in town, it was usually a month old or more, often left by a traveler passing through.

"Keep me posted," said the Sheriff as he made his way over to the Cattleman's Saloon, the premier watering hole in the small but growing town in the southwestern corner of the state between San Antonio and Del Rio. A new bank had been built on the main street and there seemed to be more strangers in town, new faces, new families, and new settlers. A sheriff keeps track of these things.

Voices carried to the street, evidence of intense talk from inside the Cattleman's. The Sheriff hesitated, briefly to listen, to get a pulse, then pushed his way into the bat-wing doors that were installed in the summer months.

"—free for the taking, I tell you! It's been that way for years," growled Garret Jones; whiskey splashing from his glass in his hand as arm's flailed. Known as Jonesy, the weathered skinny man in his forties now worked as a teamster, having lost his ranch to the new banker in town because of failure to keep up with mortgage payments.

Jones may have lost his ranch, but not his spunk thought the Sheriff as he stepped into the smoke haze that hung in the air of the busy saloon.

"Not anymore, I tell you. Ya gotta pay the Salt Ring. Them's the rules now." The speaker was a tall stranger, all of six foot four or more, dressed in a white shirt with a string tie and dark tailored pants with white pinstripes held up by a pair of leather suspenders, and the bold confident voice of a man who directed labors of others.

"No. No. Always been there. Can't just stop a man, just like you cain't make a man pay for water. Put there by the Lord, for the people. Jonesy's arms moved about excitedly, his voice now an octave higher.

Sheriff Holland's mind flashed back a few years when, as a Texas Ranger, he had been to that area referred to as the salt flats. It was a landscape of barren beauty, where dry lake beds glistened with deposits of whitened salts.

In the old days, Indians would hunt animals that were lured to the salt lick. Then the Spanish settled in the area and people from miles around would trek for days to collect salt to cure and preserve meat. When the land came under American control the Anglos sought to profit from the natural resource.

"You pay for land. Ain't free for the taking." The stranger stood his ground, moving towards the argumentative Jonesy. On his belt hung a small pocket pistol to back his play, right hand nearby. "You certainly are one who knows that. Everybody knows what happened to you and your ranch."

The words hung in the air, and the hub-bub of side talk stopped as if Jonesy had been slapped in the face. The stranger stepped in closer and continued.

"Mr. Mills put in a claim for the land at the El Paso land office. Now you gotta get a pass, and then pay for the load. You didn't pay for that last load you took. I'm here to collect." The tall stranger held out his left-hand palm up as if expecting payment, his right-hand hovering above the tiny Colt at his waist.

Jonesy's face turned red. Sweat trickled down from his forehead. There was a wheeze in his now labored breathing. A sneer showed his teeth like a rabid dog about to attack.

Sheriff Holland had seen many an argument boil over into gunplay. He stepped into the middle to separate the two hostile men, his arms nudging each farther from the other. "Jonesy, settle down now. That's enough. Step over to the bar with me."

"Noooo!" Jonesy growled and his arms thrashed as he pushed back at the Sheriff, causing the whisky from his glass to splash onto a man sitting at the card table.

"Hey! Watch it!" One of the gamblers at the card table stood quickly, hand reaching towards the still moving arms of Jonesy aiming to get the moving glass of whiskey. The man stumbled, bumping the table sending cards, money, and gold flying.

"Stop it!" Hey. That's my money!" "Them's my cards. I had a winning hand." The three other gamblers tried in vain to catch the flying gold nuggets, coins, bills, and cards.

Anger erupting, trying to stand, Jonesy's hand jerked over the gun on his hip. Men were moving, chairs falling, trying to collect their money and gold amid a mass of grunts and groans and shouts. Suddenly there was gunfire. In a flash, the Sheriff sensed that the tall stranger had drawn the tiny pocket pistol and fired at Jonesy. There were two quick bangs; more of a small pop of a .22 pocket pistol. Everyone in the Cattleman's froze in surprise.

There was a cough followed by a gurgle. Jonesy slowly sat in a nearby chair, a red circle forming on the front of his shirt while his face drained of color to a pale gray. The stranger bolted from the room disappearing out the door and around the corner of the building. Sheriff Holland took off after the man, his gimp seemingly aggravated.

Only a blood trail remained.

Chapter 2

"I got you pinned down and your horse chased off."

The sound of galloping hoofbeats and a cloud of dust were all that remained as the Sheriff rounded the corner of the Saloon. Apparently, the stranger had tied his mount out of the way at the side of the building and had escaped through a copse of cottonwoods that bordered a nearby stream. The Sheriff studied the horse-shoe prints looking again at the direction of escape, visualizing in his mind the terrain along the stream that flowed behind the saloon. He hurried off to the stable to get the roan.

The stall was empty. The hostler, Washington, was nowhere to be seen. "Washington! Where are you, man?" The sheriff walked through the stable, checking each stall for the white-colored roan with the black mane and tail. There were various horses, but not the roan. He turned towards the back corral and felt his leg, now burning in pain, nearly causing him to stumble and fall.

"Yessa, Mista Sheriff, suh. I'm here." Washington appeared, leading the roan from the back corral. The hostler, a former Buffalo Soldier with the 10th Cavalry in Kansas, knew horses better than most ranchers and cowboys. The animal was already saddled. "Suh, you're injured. Your leg. I heard gunfire and horses running. I was just bringing the roan from the back corral."

"Just a flesh wound, I gotta get this guy." The Sheriff mounted the roan, gritting his teeth as the pain raked up his leg.

"Wait, suh. You might need to bring—"

"Gotta go, trail's hot," barked the Sheriff as he jerked the reins and kicked the horse's ribs. The animal responded quickly and they were at a near-full gallop out the stable door.

The Sheriff disappeared leaving only the sound of hoofbeats. The old negro shook his head like a parent might while watching a youngin run out the door without a jacket or hat. Washington led another animal to its stall, as he chewed on a small gob of spruce tree resin, working it around in his mouth. It was a habit he learned from the Indians in his younger years with the Negro cavalry unit.

"Yessa. I'm afraid that man ain't as young as he was. Shoulda let me tend to that wound afore it festers." The old man talked to himself as he worked the treat in his mouth. "Yessa. Might be he gonna regret that decision later."

The stranger had maybe a five- or ten-minute head-start, but the roan was eager to run and kept a strong pace bounding through the creek, into the copse of trees, and westward into the prairie. Signs of a hurried trail were evident. It was easy to see the dug-in fast-moving horse-shoe marks in the ground, bentgrass, and freshly broken twigs on a Texas Sage bush. There were low rolling hills and washes making the view of the distant horizon difficult, but when a dark figure on horseback topped a distant hill a mile or two ahead, the Sheriff could see that the man was still pushing his mount.

"See 'im up there, girl? That's who we're after." On lonely rides, the Sheriff often talked to the roan. The animal answered with a snort and the Sheriff let the animal set its own pace. In the minutes that followed, he saw the rider and animal show their profile up ahead a time or two again. But careful observation suggested that in the panicked rush to flee, the rider was pushing hard and the animal was tiring. "It's just a matter of time, now."

As he rode on, the Sheriff's mind flashed back to the few moments of the incident. Jonesy had been all excited about the dispute over access to the salt deposits flats over near El Paso way. Since the days of the Indians and before, folks in the area had helped themselves to the salt that was just there for the taking on the ground near the Guadalupe mountains. And, since the loss of his ranch this past year to the bank because he had not been able to make payments on a mortgage, Jonesy had used his old wagon for hauling salt from the salt flats for folks in the area. And the argument, it appeared, was that access to the salt flats was now being controlled by some local businessman who now wanted folks to pay for the salt. It just didn't seem like a matter to be shooting folks, thought the Sheriff, as he rode in pursuit of the man who had just shot an old friend.

But there had been two shots. Jonesy had taken a bullet, but the Sheriff had not waited around to see how Jonesy was. He immediately left in pursuit of the fleeing shooter. The second .22 shot had scratched his thigh and seemed like a bee sting at the time. In the rush of an incident, adrenalin kicks in and the body reacts instinctively, often blocking any sensation of pain. A veteran of many fights and gun battles with Comanches and bandidos from back in his Rangering days, the Sheriff had once again reacted, eager for the chase, disregarding his own injury. It was nearly an hour later now, and the body's instincts had diminished and were replaced by conscious determination.

But age had taken its toll, and the body of a man in his fifties is not as spry and resilient as that of a young man in his twenties. The aches and pains were more frequent, and took longer to heal; some it seemed, never did go away. That limp from the fall off a horse many years ago seemed to renew its aching presence more often now. And the scratch of the .22 was still bleeding, its slimy warmth running down his leg and into his boot. And with each passing moment and bounce in the saddle, the pain seemed to intensify, to burn like a glowing branding iron still held in place onto his leg.

From the glimpses of the stranger on ridges up ahead, the Sheriff could see that he was closing the distance. The stranger had remained on a westerly trail, likely heading back towards El Paso. Soon, the sun was lowering into the western horizon, adding a glare that burned at the eyes. And now, as he rode up to a ridge, he saw the figure ahead walking, the horse trailing awkwardly as if lame. The Sheriff nudged the roan faster to close the gap, deciding that a straight-on approach was best.

Soon, the roan was loping up the very ridge where moments ago, the stranger had been seen walking his horse. The Sheriff scanned the nearby horizon watching for signs of his prey. There was a scattering of boulders and sagebrush along with some clumps of pinyon here and there. The hair on his neck tingled, the stranger may be waiting to bush-whack the pursuer. He reached for the Winchester, but found only an empty boot, now cursing at himself for failing to prepare, for hurrying into this ill-conceived chase. His right foot and leg were wet and the pain now came in stabs, with each bounce in the saddle.

The roan's ears twitched, and there was a bang. The Sheriff's hat flew off and he felt a sting in his scalp. Instinctively, he jumped from the saddle into a small gully that ran along the roadway here, finding a small boulder to use as a shield. A second shot splattered near the feet of the roan causing the horse to turn and run away. But the muzzle flash revealed the location of the shooter. The Sheriff braced his colt on the boulder, squinted at the front site, and squeezed a shot just behind the spot of the muzzle flash.

He heard a yelp and a curse. After just a moment, he called out. "This here is Sheriff Clay Holland of Bent Creek. Throw out our gun and come on out of there. Your horse is lame and I've got you pinned down."

"Ha! I got you pinned down and your horse chased off."

"I got all day. You're mine. Give it up."

"Come and get me!" The remark was punctuated with a shot.

The Sheriff just ducked. But the little bit of movement shot pain from the bullet wound in his leg. Sweat was dripping into his eyes and running down his neck onto his back. Now, he was getting thirsty. Blood loss makes a man dry and thirsty. He remembered that he hadn't even brought a canteen. The sun beat relentlessly and was dropping lower towards the ground. The Sheriff picked up a pebble and rubbed the dust from it, then put it under his tongue. In a moment, he began to salivate, just a bit.

"It's just a matter of time. You're mine. You burned out your horse and now you've burned out your luck. Give it up." The Sheriff was trying to wear down his will and make him want to give up.

"I'm walking away."

"Give it up. Ya shot a man in the saloon in front of witnesses"

"He drew on me. Y'all saw it."

"And now you're shooting at a lawman. Give it up. Ya don't gotta die here today. Come back with me, get a fair trial."

The man answered with another shot that ricocheted off the boulder spitting a bit of rock into the Sheriff's face. Now the shadows were getting long and the red sun sat on the western horizon like a great gleaming tomato. He knew he had to wrap this up soon or lose his prey in the darkness. There was little moon and the night would be dark. A careful man could make his escape into the west Texas desert.

His mind flashed back to the day two years ago when he had caught up with outlaw Josiah Judd, the man who had killed his wife some years before. That chase had crossed many miles of the state, ending up in a stand-off much like the present situation. That man too had refused to give up, replying with shots when offered an opportunity for a trial. The Sheriff had been able to sneak over and make a flanking attack to catch and kill a man who had left a trail of crime and dead and wounded before being stopped by bullets from the Sheriff's gun.

Time wore on. The sun's glare was now a brilliant orange. The few scattered clouds could not temper the stifling heat. The Sheriff scanned left and right, looking for a way to sneak around to the side or behind this man who, truth be told, had the upper hand at the moment. Currently behind a lone bolder along the roadway, and little growth save for a few mesquite bushes, there was no easy way to sneak around and get the drop on this weasel. The only choice was to crawl along in the gully, which likely would make him an exposed target. But sitting still and waiting worked to the advantage of the stranger who could sneak away in the darkness.

The Sheriff remembered the Indian wars, where the sly Comanches could sneak up to the Ranger's defensive position by crawling in ankle-high field grass and popping up suddenly to charge from just a few feet away. He found a few rocks and flung them over behind the position where the stranger had holed up behind a large boulder looking down over the roadway. As the rocks tinkled against the hillside behind, the stranger reacted with a gasp and a wild shot to his rear. It was just enough diversion that the Sheriff was able to crawl snake-like down the gully to a bunch of pinyons. It took a few minutes; slowly he inched along keeping flat, breathing the dusty soil.

Finally, he pulled himself up behind the pinyons. Once there, he waited as shadows crossed the road giving some hint of darkness to come and an opportunity to cross the road and approach the stranger in a flanking position. Once across, the Sheriff snuck forward behind some sagebrush. He picked up two rocks and again threw them over behind the stranger's position. The startled movement confirmed that the stranger was still in the position behind the boulder and had not escaped.

"You not fooling me throwing them rocks," called out the stranger.

The Sheriff bit his lip, holding back from answering, not wanting to disclose his flanking approach. Just a couple more steps, crouched, quietly.

He spun his cylinder, ejected a spent shell, and inserted another live cartridge. Just through the sagebrush, he could see the man squatting uncomfortably getting ready to make his move.   The Sheriff stood, Colt cocked and ready.

"Hold it right there. Don't move or you're a dead man. Drop that rifle!"

Chapter 3

"...Mills send you here to collect a tariff?"

The man swung the rifle around and the Sheriff responded with a bullet, hitting the man's shoulder causing the rifle to discharge harmlessly before it was dropped. In three quick steps, the Sheriff had the rifle out of reach of the wounded man.

"You're under arrest," said the Sheriff.

"You can't arrest me. He drew on me," pleaded the man as he grimaced in pain, a bloodied hand holding his wounded shoulder.

"Tell it to the judge. You'll get your day in court for that. I'm arresting you for attempted murder of a peace officer."

The prisoner had only given his first name, Darrel, but had refused to answer any questions during the walk back to Bent Creek. The Sheriff rode the roan behind the tethered prisoner and his lame mount. It was well after midnight when the Sheriff walked his captured quarry into town. Even the Cattleman's Saloon was dark and quiet.

At the clicking of horse hoofs, Washington appeared from the darkness of the stable and took the reins of the animals while the Sheriff tended to his prisoner. Just as the prisoner was settling into his cell, there was a knock and Doc appeared at the door of the Sheriff's office and jail.

"Clay? Let me take a look at that leg. Should have let me patch you up before you went after that man. Miss Betsy, she fit to be tied with worry, you running off like that."

Feeling weak and exhausted, the Sheriff slumped into his chair without argument. One hand reached into the bottom drawer for the bottle of whiskey that was stored there. The nearly empty bottle went straight to his lips and was downed in two gulps.

"Hold still. Hold still. This is gonna sting." Doc had ripped away the bloodied pant leg and was wiping away the dirt and blood. "Ya got so much dirt in here it helped stop the hemorrhaging. Mighta saved your life."

"Oowe! Easy there, Doc. Where's that other bottle?"

The door burst open and Betsy Brown flowed in, swishing her long dress and petticoats as she leaned in to examine the wounded sheriff. Her robust bosoms dangled near his face; a flowery perfume filled the air. "Clay! Clay, you all right? You shouldna run off like that!"

"Wull, Miss Betsy, I'm just doing my job." While the Sheriff disliked the idea of being the center of attention with folks hovering about, he quickly warmed up to the attention from the comely and curvaceous proprietor of the Red-eye Saloon. "Now Betsy dear, long as you here, can you fetch me that bottle from the cabinet in the back room?"

By mid-afternoon, Miss Betsy had delivered a late breakfast to the Sheriff and his prisoner. Doc had patched up the prisoner's wounds after first tending to his friend. In the daylight, the man looked young, maybe mid-twenties, and did not appear as cocky as he had the day before arguing with Jonesy in the Cattleman's. Rather, he looked more like a young kid in over his head. The Sheriff used the opportunity of warm savory vittles to soften up the detainee for a few questions.

"Now, Darrell. Last night you told me your name was Darrell, but you neglected to give me a last name. Let's have it."

"Uh, hmm." The young man finished wiping up some gravy on a piece of bread, finishing the meal, and wiping his lips on the unbandaged sleeve of his right arm. "Peterson, Sir. Darrel Peterson."

"And you work for Mills, over El Paso way? Collecting a tariff on the salt?"

"That's right."

"Did Mills send you here to collect a tariff from our man Jonesy?"

"Yes, he did. That man Jones was told he needed to pay, but he stormed off pitching a fit. He came back later and scooped up a load and left without paying." The young man's confidence and cocky attitude were growing as he talked about Jonesy.

The Sheriff chewed on a toothpick, thinking for a moment. "Is it posted,…that you gotta pay now? You got proof he took a load?

"Well, yeh, it's posted there by the road. He stole the salt."

"You got proof? Proof he stole any salt?"

"Well, no, cause he didn't pay. If'n he'd a paid, he'd a had a receipt. Why don't you ask him?" the man flared.

"Jonesy died. Ya killed him. He can't tell us anything."

Chapter 4

"I'd like you to meet Miss Clara Williams, the new teacher."

The leg still hurt, but Sheriff Clay Holland knew that the body healed faster by getting up and around. By exercising and using sore muscles the body repairs itself more quickly. After his second day on the mend from his leg wound, he insisted on walking down to the Red-eye for breakfast.

The Red-eye was busy this morning, but the Sheriff found his usual table kept open by proprietor Betsy Brown. There were several journals, pencils, and writing paper. As the Sheriff took a seat, he observed a group of people in a far corner talking excitedly. He noted that the group was mostly ladies. One of the servers brought him a coffee and confirmed his breakfast order.

"Well good morning Clay. I'm glad to see that you are up and about." Betsy met her favorite customer with a big smile. Just then a pretty and prim young lady nervously stepped around from behind Betsy, her arms protectively crossed at her front showing an expectant smile on an attractive creamy complexion.

"Clay, I'd like you to meet Miss Clara Williams. Miss Williams is the new teacher for Bent Creek. We're so excited to have her." Betsy was beaming with pride as if the young lady were her own daughter.

Young Maria, the run-away girl child adopted by Betsy arrived with the breakfast order and set the steaming plate of steak and eggs in front of the sheriff. Seeing the teacher standing there, the young girl lowered her head in embarrassment and turned to return to the kitchen.

"Maria, one minute, uhm, *un minuto*. I'd like you to meet the new teacher, Miss Williams," said Betsy.

Maria smiled shyly and glanced down at the floor once again. The Sheriff sat back amused and watched the interaction.

"Oh my. What a pretty girl, you have such pretty eyes and dark shiny hair," the teacher gushed. "How old are you?"

The young girl flushed in embarrassment at the attention. Betsy spoke on behalf of her new kitchen helper in the Saloon. "She just learning to speak English, and I'm learning to speak Mexican. Uhm, *¿cuántos años?*"

"Tengo nueve años," I'm nine years old said the little girl.

"And where is our new teacher from?" asked the Sheriff, allowing the girl to get out of the lime-light and disappear back into the kitchen.

"I'm from Louisville, Kentucky. I graduated from the University of Louisville last year," said the young lady in her mid-twenties. She wiped her damp face in response to the heat and humidity of the Texas summer. "I'm so excited to be here. Is it always this hot here?"

"Well, welcome to Texas," said the Sheriff. "Our summers tend to be stifling, but winters tend to be milder than the northern states. I haven't heard of a schoolhouse being built. Where are you going to be conducting classes?"

"Uhm, I've been told that we'll be conducting classes at a ranch house south of town.," said Miss Williams, her brow wrinkled in uncertainty.

"I can answer that." The new voice in the conversation was Harlan Hawkins, the new banker in town. "The Bent Creek Bank is making a property available for the benefit of the children of the town. "Several of the other women in the Red-eye had turned their attention to the group now gathered around the Sheriff's table. Hawkins was an operator in business deals and social interactions. Seeing that he had the upper hand at the moment, he sought to take further advantage of the opportunity.

"And that would be...?" The Sheriff was on edge with this man, having had some issues with the business deals that came about when the bank began construction in Bent Creek.

"That would be the Jones place, "said Hawkins. "Pardon me, Miss Williams. My name is Harlan Hawkins., President of the Bent Creek Bank. The man was well dressed and smooth, his voice exuding confidence and charm. He bowed gallantly and touched the hand of the young teacher.

"The Jones' place? I should have known," The Sheriff's remark came out as a growl reflecting his anger over the business transaction that caused Jonesy to lose his ranch to the bank. The animosity between Hawkins and the Sheriff was mutual.

Hawkins ignored the Sheriff's comment and spoke quickly. "It was our organization that arranged for you to come to town. There's space there for your residence and, of course, for the schoolroom. And we're negotiating for added property and will be building a new schoolhouse in town by next year."

The young teacher was embarrassed at being the center of attention of the group in her newly adopted town. Hawkins now had the attention of the women in the Red-eye and took full advantage of the interested audience. "Miss Williams, I have the carriage, and I'd be happy to give you a ride out there, show you around."

Chapter 5

"Started with St. Elmo's Fire, that eerie glow on the horns..."

A summer storm had passed through overnight, one of those furious prairie squalls with harsh winds, exploding flashes of lightning, and a cannonade of thunder stirring animals and humans alike to fear and fright. Throughout the blackness of night, howling winds shook doors and rattled windows. A tree fell damaging a backyard shed, and across town, a strong burst of wind culminated in the crashing sound of a windmill blown down splintering into pieces.

Finally, the winds settled, the rain stopped, and the sky edged to a morning gray. Then a brilliant yellow sun peeked over the passing cloud front revealing downed trees, ponds in the fields, puddles of brown muddy goop in the street, and the collapsed windmill structure blocking the western access to town. The fierce roaring winds had blown the Cattleman's Saloon sign from the building's front and laid it at the entrance of the cemetery on the eastern edge of town. Every building in town showed some signs of the night storm's brutality. Only the newly constructed Bent Creek Bank building seemed unscathed.

The morning saw Bent Creek citizens venturing forth cautiously, surveying their properties for damage. Most found parts of lumber or facing blown from buildings and began picking up blown items and wooden tools left out. Others worked at repairing building walls or roofs where wind and water had caused damage.

At the Cattleman's Saloon, barkeep Sam had spent part of the morning sweeping broken shards of glass from broken whiskey bottles blown from their shelves by the force of the wind shaking the wooden structure that sat on piers, not held in place by a stone foundation.

Drinkers trickled in, looking disheveled and sleepless, anxious for a whiskey to calm the nerves. Even Leverett Brockton III, the house gambler, sat numbly at a table off to the side, whiskey bottle in one hand and glass in the other with no cards in sight. After several drinks, nerves calmed and veterans of Texas civil war cavalry regiments shared stories about the bolts of lightning and booming of thunder causing flashbacks to days in battle at Shiloh, Gettysburg, and Chickamauga.

"Tornado. It was a tornado. I saw the downward tail of a cloud in the lightning flashes." Smith Ranch Foreman Buck Carroll had come in, his clothes still damp and splattered in mud. He gestured for a drink and Sam obliged. Everyone in the saloon stopped talking and turned to hear a first-hand account. He leaned back and took a mouthful, wiping his lips on a muddy sleeve.

"Started with St. Elmo's Fire, that eerie glow on the horns. I could see it from the ranch house, a quarter-mile away." Buck's eyes flashed as he recalled the images of the night before. "Then the wind kicked up, throwing dirt 'n' dust, blowing so hard we couldn't get out to save the cattle. In the lightning flashes, I saw that tail from the cloud. It just missed the herd. They were running, but the storm picked up several critters and flung them like the popper on a whip."

"I could hear them bawling through the wind as they ran. Scared shit-less, every one of 'em." Buck finished the glass of whiskey in a second gulp. "The whole herd now is remnants and strays, scattered all over the north sector. It'll take us a week to round 'em up again. Anybody looking for work, week or two, I'm heading out from the McCann's Mercantile in thirty minutes."

Buck turned and was headed out the door; he had work to do. He gave a nod to Sheriff Holland who had walked in mid-way through the story. A buzz of conversation began immediately as men began talking all at once. Only the word "tornado" could be heard as everyone reacted to the story. Two cowboys finished their drinks and followed Buck out the door.

By the time the Sheriff had reached the bar, a glass of whiskey was waiting for him. He nodded in appreciation to Sam and set a coin on the bar.

"I saw your sign down the street," he commented to Sam.

"I wondered where it went." Sam was wiping down the bar with a cloth. "It was all I could do to get the place cleaned up before guys were coming in. I had five or six bottles blown off the shelves, all busted up. The wind was shaking the place so bad."

The Sheriff smirked, erupting into chuckles. "Well, your sign's right at the entrance of the boot hill. Kind of ominous, really. Might be bad for business. In your spare time, otta drag it back before it scares away your customers."

It was two days before the puddles had evaporated and soppy mud hardened into rutted clay on the roadways. Gradually, daily lives around Bent Creek returned to normal. A work crew was putting finishing touches on the new bank, initially focusing on the exterior checking for storm damage. Late in the day, a freight wagon arrived pulled by a team of six draft horses. The wagon was heavy-duty and carried its freight covered by a large tarp. The covered item appeared to be six or seven feet tall, shaped kind of like an outhouse, well more like six outhouses, about the size of a one-room cabin.

The Sheriff stepped out of his office, noticing the heavy clinks and rattles that gave recollection of a horse-drawn artillery battery. He watched as Harlan Hawkins emerged from the bank, looking the role of a banker with pinstriped woolen slacks, a starched white shirt sporting an upstanding collar pressed into wings with a string bow tie and bands on the sleeves. The teamster led the banker over to the wagon and tugged on the tarp covering the freight. They peeked under the tarp, and then the men talked animatedly with gestures and pointing.

"What is happening Sheriff suh?" Washington had walked over from the stable to observe the activity across the street.

"Damned if I know, Washington," replied the Sheriff. "A big parcel for the bank. From the looks of that wagon and those horses, it must be heavy. Brings to mind one of those artillery units in the war between the states."

"Yessa, suh, I seen them artillery batteries. Yessa, last night sounded just like them artillery guns blasting away. Them horses was mighty nervous last night."

The men watched as the wagon was positioned next to a side door to the bank. The teamster then began to pull out some timbers and positioned them vertically into slots framed inside the heavy-duty wagon. Then angled and cross-piece timbers were fitted and attached. Finally, the teamster climbed up on his sturdily constructed tower and attached a block and tackle like those used when ships were loaded and unloaded at the port. A chain was wrapped around the room-sized parcel. The second teamster had unhitched one of the draft horses and walked it around to the side of the wagon. The chain was fastened to the animals' rigging. At a signal, the chain-connected draft horse was walked forward, tugging the chain through the block and tackle causing the heavy load to be lifted up over the sidewalls of the wagon. The wind blew at the tarp revealing the heavy item.

"It's a safe. They're delivering a large walk-in safe to store the money in the bank," commented the Sheriff.

"Yessa. Keep them valuables safe and secure," said Washington as he turned and went back to the stable to tend to the horses.

A few of the other workmen were summoned by Hawkins and enlisted to help move the heavy safe of some small wheels through the door. Once inside, other workers began framing the side entrance and adding siding, closing off the side door so that it appeared like the regular wall of the bank. A worker began painting the newly closed-off wall as the teamsters came out from the bank and dismantled the tower structure storing the beams in the wagon. The team of draft horses was turned and ye-haa-ed out of town back east towards San Antonio.

When the Sheriff returned from the Red-eye after dinner he saw that posters had been nailed to various porch rails and trees around town. The signs read:

"Grand Opening
Welcome one and all to visit the Bent Creek Bank
Opening Monday 9:00 AM Sharp.
Harlan Hawkins, President"

Chapter 6

A four-man band began playing, starting with Dixie...

Monday morning promised to be another hot one. Across the street, the new bank building had been festooned with red, white, and blue banners from the railings, porches, and under each window on the first and second floors. The building looked all dressed up for Independence Day although the holiday had been celebrated several weeks prior. Led by Betsy Brown, ladies from the Red-eye Saloon were carrying trays of food-stuffs from their kitchen down the street to be offered to the visitors to the Bank's grand opening celebration. The Red-eye had been retained by Harlan Hawkins to supply food treats for the grand opening event.

"Excellent! Excellent Betsy. Those look delicious." Ever the gentleman with the ladies, Harlan Hawkins gushed, giving a broad smile and a wink to each of the ladies. "Over here please, on these tables. What do we have here?"

The charm of this southern gentleman seemed to give Betsy's heart a quiver. Her cheeks flushed and her eyes fluttered revealing her unspoken pleasure at having received the approval from this handsome well-dressed man. The server girls from the Red-eye enjoyed the man's attention and did their best to gain his attention. They had quibbled over who would get the opportunity to participate in this catering job and deliver the steaming food to the bank. In the end, Betsy had to referee her staff, selecting those three who had produced the best dishes. The winners had been working through the night so that a large volume of portable food would be ready for delivery in the morning.

Betsy carried shredded beef sandwiches in a tomato-flavored bar-b-que sauce, cut to small finger sizes. "Cookie" Cora carried cut chicken pieces, some flavored with sweet butter and others in the tomato bar-b-que sauce. The trim thirty-year-old had earned her nickname because of her silly sense of humor and flavorful sugar cookies offered as dessert at the Red-eye. Blonde-haired Hilda, a plump middle-aged lady with a strong German accent, carried her favorite dish, a still steaming baked apple pie.

"Set the plates here, please." Harlan Hawkins fawned over each plate as the ladies placed their dishes on the serving table, with a charming smile and a comment about the dish or the lady's appearance.

"Here, try mine first." "Oh, Mr. Hawkins, you must try this special sauce. You'll just love it." "Oh my! Oh my! I have a sweet cookie treat just for you." "You must taste zees hot apple pie, Herr Hawkins." The ladies competed for his attention.

Savoring the attention, Hawkins accepted an offered taste by each, licking his lips and mumbling a "hmm-hmm" with each taste. Moments later when the ladies were looking around, awed by the decorative interior of the new bank building, Hawkins wrinkled his nose and tossed the remainder of uneaten morsels out an open side window where a couple of dogs had gathered enticed by the wafting food aromas.

Outside on the porch, a four-man band had begun playing, starting with "Dixie" and moving on to "Bonnie Blue Flag" and the "The Yellow Rose of Texas." The band looked to be former civil war soldiers in old army tunics over their civilian clothes. Three were in Confederate butternut and one wore a Union blue cavalry coat sporting brass buttons and bars of an officer. One tapped the beat on a marching style snare drum, while another worked a fiddle and two blew the curved Sax horns, thumping their feet to the beat. The bank open house was going all out with the grand opening celebration.

It was working, because as the music began playing, people filled the street, streaming out from the buildings and saloons in town. Riders and wagons appeared, finding open hitches to tie their mounts. Many stood around, watching the band and the festivities. Sheriff Holland emerged from his office and stood across the street near his doorway watching the people and festivities, unaware that his right foot had begun tapping to the beat of the band.

After a few moments, Harlan Hawkins appeared at the doorway to the bank, holding open the sturdily built white-washed oak door with the arched windows. He signaled to the band to stop playing and then called out to the growing crowd of lookers.

"Do come in for a tour. And please partake of the fabulous repast that has been prepared by the fair ladies of our town. Come see the new Bent Creek Bank. See our strong and secure new safe, perfect for storage of your new valuables."

The new teacher, Miss Clara Williams appeared at the door wearing an ankle-length flowered print cotton dress. She stepped out, standing next to Hawkins. She seemed to speak into his ear and they appeared to have a brief but lively conversation. Hawkins called out again to the crowd.

"Come in and meet our new teacher, direct from Louisville, Kentucky. Beginning next month, there will be classes for all the children. I introduce you to Miss Clara Williams."

There was polite applause from the assembling crowd. Surprised by the introduction, Miss Williams flushed. But she pushed an errant strand of brown hair behind her ear and did her best to step forward. "Thank you. Thank you, Mister Hawkins. As you know, my name is Miss Clara Williams. I will be teaching all the children, primary grades up to eighth grade. All are welcome. We will be studying reading, writing, and arithmetic. And yes, the social studies, a look at the great war, and the constitution test. Classes will be at what has been called the Jones Place."

This time, there was an enthusiastic round of applause and the drummer did a four-tap- salute for the attractive young teacher causing laughter from the crowd and more applause. The band began another round of "Dixie," and the throng began to enter the brightly festooned bank building.

Sheriff Holland followed the milling crowd through the door of the fresh-smelling cream-colored interior of the newly constructed bank. He watched the people enter, look around in awe, and greet their friends and neighbors, chatting excitedly.

Upon entering, the throng encountered a long table covered with a white table cloth and large steaming serving plates with beef sandwiches, bar-b-que chicken pieces, cookies, and apple pie. Behind each serving dish stood the creators from the Red-eye Saloon, wearing glowing smiles, a white apron, holding a serving fork, and offering a small plate of their baked cuisine. The titter of voices was friendly and excited, looking about at the decorative bunting inside, several large framed paintings of the American West, wall-mounted candle sconces, oak desks in each corner, and a high ceiling framed with crown molding from which hung three twinkling candle-lit chandeliers.

Along the back wall stood a chest-high stained oak counter, looking much like the bar from the Cattleman's Saloon, absent the brass foot rail. Standing behind the counter were two bank tellers, middle-aged men in starched white shirts with string ties and sleeve bands, much the same style as bank president Harlan Hawkins. Behind the teller counter, the large room-sized vault stood, with its heavy iron door swung open revealing shelves and metal boxes inside.

Harlan Hawkins seemed to be everywhere, greeting each visitor as if they were a guest in his home. Effortlessly, he elicited the guest's name, their spouse and children's names, and the family occupation or business, ending with smiling encouragement that the individual take advantage of the secure services of Bent Creek Bank by depositing their hard-earned funds.

As the Sheriff moved about watching the activity with a lawman's eye. He patiently waited in line until he had Betsy's undivided attention, complimenting her on the fine vittles and chatting momentarily. He continued along the serving line greeting the Red-eye ladies and accepting a sample of the apple pie from Hilda. From outside the bank building, movement caught his eye, and the hair rose on the back of his neck. Something gray? The Sheriff quickly exited the crowded building to confront what he senses as a possible threat.

Chapter 7

The man leaned in trying to shoulder past the Sheriff.

The boardwalk in front of the bank was congested as people moved past each other, some entering as others exited the bank building. There was laughter and talk as neighbors greeted each other at this now festive event. The Sheriff squeezed by, out to the street, and looked around trying to find the movement that had caught the corner of his eye. Was it a gray coat or a gray saddle blanket? There were a few horses in the street, but none with gray saddle blankets. Of the people milling about, there were none dressed in gray; even the retired soldiers providing the music wore the butternut tan-colored tunics. He headed back across the street to his office.

Upon arriving at his office, a man stepped forward from around the corner. He was a middle-aged citified looking man dressed in a gray suit and vest with a small bowler hat. He glared at the sheriff, his eyes settling on the brass star pinned to the Sheriff's chest.

"Are you the Sheriff? Sheriff Holland? I need a word with you. Let's step into your office." He was a chunky man with a thick mop of dark hair. His baritone voice carried confidence, expecting compliance.

"And you are…?" The Sheriff held his ground, even though the man was taller. "I don't believe we've met."

"Of course. My name is Charles Broward, attorney–at–law. I'm here to secure the release of my man, Peterson. You've got him locked up."

"Yes, I do. And he's not going anywhere," bristled the Sheriff. "He killed a man and failed in his efforts to kill me. He's awaiting trial."

"I'm the man's attorney. I'm prepared to cover his bond. He's needed for his job in El Paso." The man had his hand on the doorknob of the Sheriff's office demonstrating a clear intent to enter.

"No! Peterson is not going anywhere. He's my prisoner." The Sheriff stepped to block the attorney's access to the doorway.

The man then leaned in trying to shoulder past the Sheriff. It was obvious that this Charles Broward was accustomed to pushing his weight around. The Sheriff likewise leaned into the aggressive visitor like two buck deer locking horns in rutting season. The push went back and forth, and again, each testing the other. Muscles tensed, breathing intensified. And then there was a "click."

"Back off or you're a dead man, Broward." The Sheriff pushed the Colt up into the man's gut. "You're like no attorney I've ever seen before."

The attorney then stepped back, his hands coming up in front of his chest, ending the pushing contest. A guilty smirk showed on his face.

"I'm from Missouri, kind sir, on behalf of my client. I'm sure we can come to some sort of agreeable compromise." The smooth baritone gave no hint of the physical altercation moments before. "He is a valuable asset that is sorely needed on the premises in El Paso. I give you my word as an attorney that my client will present himself upon summons by the court."

"Your man killed one of Bent Creek's citizens. He stays here."

"Such allegation has yet to be proven in a court of law, kind sir."

The Sheriff's anger was growing. "Such murder happened in my presence. And his second bullet went through my leg. Then he fled. Innocent men don't flee. Upon my pursuit, he attempted to bush-whack me. For these reasons he stays here where I can keep an eye on him and make sure that he attends his trial.

"Perhaps sir, we can come to terms." Charles Broward reached into the pocket in his vest and retrieved a roll of bills that riffled like a small paper fan as the roll un-wound.

"Are you trying to bribe a Texas officer of the law?"

"A financial bond, sir to guarantee his return for court upon summons, a practice which is observed in the states east of the grand ole Mississippi," Charles Broward persisted.

"Get the hell out of my town!" barked the Sheriff, as he gestured towards the western edge of town with his Colt.

"All right, all right." The money had disappeared and the man's hands arose in defeat in front of his chest. "But I would like to have a word with my client. Surely you cannot forbid a man to the opportunity to confer with his counsel."

"You've got five minutes. Give me any and all weapons on your person. Me and Samuel Colt will be waiting in the outside office."

Charles Broward reached under his coat and pulled out his own Colt .44, spinning the weapon downward and extending the handle to the Sheriff. The Sheriff then opened the door and let the attorney enter and talk to his client. The Sheriff stood waiting at his desk in the front of the office. There was some whispering, and then a chuckle, and the attorney came around the corner.

"Thank you, kind sir. Here is my card. I trust you will keep me informed when the court date is scheduled so that I may be present to defend my client.

The following day, the Sheriff encountered a familiar face sipping on a whiskey standing at the bar in the Cattleman's Saloon.

"Deever! What brings you to town?" the Sheriff asked as bartender Sam placed a glass on the bar for his best regular customer.

"Uh, howdy, Sheriff Holland. I been riding the north range for Mr. Smith, gathering up them strays from that tornado last week," Deever replied. "Um, thank you for asking Mr. Smith to take me on as a hand. That's a mighty big ranch he got up there."

"You're a good hand, your work speaks for itself. You did good work when you worked for Jonesy. All I done was make an introduction," replied the Sheriff.

"Yeh, and I get to town and hear that Jonesy was shot up on accounta he be hauling salt from El Paso. You get the man that done that?"

"Yep, he's cooling his heels in the lock-up at my office."

Just then rancher James Smith came into the Cattleman's and joined his new hand. "Mornin' Clay. Deever, we'll be loaded in ten minutes, I'll look for you outside."

"Yes sir, Mr. Smith." Deever finished his whiskey and dutifully headed for the door.

Smith watched his new cowhand walk out the door, and nodded as Sam placed a glass of the rancher's special Tennessee bourbon on the bar. He turned to his former ranger partner and now Bent Creek Sheriff. "I hear tell you been busy. Captured the fellow that shot Jonesy."

"Yep. Tried to bushwhack me." The Sheriff washed down his drink. "I went all Comanche on him, crawled along a dry wash, and flanked him.".

"Ranger skills. Once learned, they never leave you," observed Smith with a nod of approval.

"Say, James, what do you know about a fellow name of Charles Broward?"

"Well, I hear tell he's a player in the salt wars over El Paso way. Some call him district attorney, others call him a judge. I call him an operator. He's trying to lay claim to land over on the salt flats so's he can charge a fee to them that come for some salt." As a former ranger captain and now a prominent rancher in the Bent Creek area, James Smith kept a pulse of politics in Austin and law enforcement efforts in the area.

The glass tinkled and whiskey gurgled as Sam refilled the drinks for both men as they stood at the bar talking.

The Sheriff continued. "Yep, apparently this Broward fella sent one Darrell Peterson to town here to collect a fee from Jonesy for his last load of salt. Led to gunplay, killing Jonesy. So, I got Peterson, and just yesterday, this Broward fella shows up and says he's an attorney and he's trying to buy freedom for his man."

"You didn't---"

"No way in hell! I gave him five minutes with his man and then told him to light a shuck."

Smith nodded in approval. He heard a whistle outside, finished his Tennessee whiskey, and gave the Sheriff a brotherly punch in the shoulder as he headed out the door.

Chapter 8

The López brothers ran the streets of Laredo learning a life of crime.

The fire flared from a gust of wind and the smoke circled blowing embers towards the two men who had just shifted their position because of smoke in their eyes. In the darkness along the tree line in a stand of cottonwoods a few feet away, their horses snorted and stamped nervously, fearful of smoke and crackling flames.

"Ya just can't get away from the smoke, ya know?" Junior López said, his voice high-pitched like that of a whining child. Scruffy with a dirt-stained babyface, at age fifteen, he was the youngest of the López brothers. "Where's Ronnie? Said he'd be here by sundown. He shoulda been here two hours ago."

"Quit yer bitchin', hermano Bebe. Ronnie will be here when he gets here." Tommie López, the middle brother, had a perpetual disdain for his baby brother; the two older brothers always referring to the little one as baby brother, Hermano Bebe.

Somewhere in the darkness of the south Texas plains, a coyote howled to the night. It was followed by the howl of a second animal, this one closer to the campfire. The picketed horses stirred nervously.

"Oh, I hate that sound. Them coyotes closin' in on us," mumbled Bebe as he squinted into the darkness.

"Yeh, they want to eat your juicy tender body. Jest shut up and the fire will keep them away," growled Tommie.

The López brothers shared facial features that observers quickly recognized them as brothers, with their thick mop of dirty dark hair, prominent nose and chin, and a perpetual angry scowl. Appearing unstylishly similar in hand-me-down home-spun peon garments with ground- in brown Texas dirt, it made their light-skinned faces stand out among the border population. Their light skin was attributed to their mother, Anita Anders who had married Renaldo López, a civil war deserter from the north side of Rio Bravo. Renaldo had abandoned their American-born mother shortly after the birth of the third baby, named Junior. The older brothers had called Junior Hermano Bebe.

The López brothers ran the streets of Laredo learning a life of crime as barefoot waifs. They grew into young men with thick necks, scarred bodies, and solid muscles. They were always together, always in trouble, or creating trouble. They grew up to be real scrappers, dirty fighters when squabbles escalated, starting a fight with fists and ending it with some hidden weapon or broken bottle. The firstborn, called Ronnie, had a reputation as a fast gun anxious to take on local toughs as they passed from town to town. Over the years, their reputation had spread through Texas from the southern shores to the *llano estacado*.

"I'm hungry," wined Bebe, the runt of the litter. "He better bring some food, or else."

"Or else what? What you gonna do Bebe?" It was a deep voice from the darkness outside the small ring of light given off by the flickering campfire.

"Ronnie? Is that you?" Bebe jumped up and spun around looking into the darkness. "You bring food?"

"Yeh, but you ain't getting' any. You're careless, sitting in front of that fire like a moth. You get nothing 'till you cut some more firewood and picket this horse. Give him a rubdown too."

"Oh, man, I'm hungry Ronnie." A runt of the family, Bebe grumbled, but always did what he was told.

"Git along. Me and Tommie got a job to talk about. Food will be ready when you get back." Ronnie lit a cigarette and sat on a log next to Tommie. "We got a bank job. I heard tell in town there's a new bank opening up in a little town called Bent Creek."

"What? I ain't never heard of it. Can't be all that big. You sure they got money up there?" Tommie was a follower, but he had the sense to ask questions, to think things out, and did it in a way that Ronnie did not feel threatened by his younger brother. Just a year apart, they could pass for twins. Sometimes they tried to pull scams with travelers or storekeepers with each playing the role of a customer or traveler, one being friendly and the other being threatening or angry or mean. Both rode similar-looking duns.

"How'd you hear about this?" asked Tommie.

"I got a tip from a friend. It's up on the westerly road from San Antone. Some big shot banker from out east built new bank in town, the talk of west Texas." Ronnie was the leader.

"But a new bank, maybe they ain't got no money yet," cautioned Tommie.

"Oh, they got money all right. Talk of the town is that the banker brought money from the east, and he's making big promises to the local folk." Ronnie would hang out in the dark corners of the saloons to hear what was going on, to find new opportunities for taking from those who had property or horses or money.

Tommie persisted. "But a new bank, it's gonna have a new concrete and steel vaults, don't ya think?"

"Yeh, but I got a plan." Ronnie turned and called into the darkness where the horses were tethered. "Hey, Bebe. Get over here with that firewood. Put on the coffee and the frijoles. I got us some venison."

Chapter 9

She wore riding britches with riding boots and sat on a horse like a man.

The man was meticulous in appearance, but temperamentally anxious and high-strung, much like the white Arabian show horse that he rode. And demanding, the man was always demanding special attention, making a big issue out of the daily adversities of life on the Texas prairie. These were the thoughts that ran through the Sheriff's mind as he rode southward back towards town after another visit to the McDonald ranch to investigate a complaint about stock rustling.

There were common events that happened to every rancher such as a broken fence, escaped animals, or finding an animal carcass that had been hunted and consumed by coyotes leaving only remnants for the turkey vultures. But sheep rancher Donald McDonald seemed to view these issues as personal attacks rather than recognizing such events as nature's way and taking life in stride. Consequently, the man's excited complaints about property damage and theft of stock soon became frequent demands for an investigation, only to reveal that footprint evidence revealed natural events.

Outside of confronting the occasional gun-wielding outlaw, dealing with drunks in the saloons and rustling complaints were the main bread and butter of a small-town Sheriff's daily activity. So, the ride out to investigate the sheep rustling complaint of sheep rancher McDonald, had turned out to be a pleasant day for a ride in the country even with the sticky Texas humidity.

The roan had set its own pace for the return trip. Movement on the side of a nearby knoll caught the Sheriff's eye. It was a yellow-breasted tan bird squawking, circling low to the ground and diving down, then circling again. It was a meadowlark. From behind a stand of bunch grama grass, a fox pup jumped, followed by a second pup. The small pups with big ears cowered as the squawking bird dove again. Then it became clear as a tan baby bird hopped away in the opposite direction. The fox pups were practicing hunting skills, having found a fledging meadowlark, but the momma bird fought to protect her young.

The roadway curved around the knoll and revealed a young woman standing silently alongside a chestnut gelding. She seemed spellbound, watching something on the side of the hill. The Sheriff's eyes followed the sightline, recognizing that the young lady had been watching the same confrontation between the meadowlark and the fox pups. He steered the roan in her direction.

She wore riding britches with riding boots, and she sat on a horse like a man, legs straddling the animal's midsection, unlike the common practice for women to ride side-saddle. Her broad-brimmed straw hat with a colorful silk scarf secured the hat around her neck.

"Life's lesson played out before your very eyes," the Sheriff commented just as the gelding reacted to the presence of the roan and its rider.

"Wha,…Oh my! You startled me." It was Clara Williams, the new school teacher.

"Let me offer one more life lesson," said the Sheriff. "West Texas prairie is still a wild land, and a bandido with bad intentions could have surprised you. You must stay alert to your surroundings. What brings you out this way?"

"Oh, you're Sheriff Holland. We met at the Red-eye. This is such a beautiful country, so wide open. There were more trees in Kentucky. I was just exploring. And then I heard this ruckus, that squawking bird, and I saw those little puppies."

"Those are fox puppies, wild animals testing their hunting skills. Their mama is around somewhere nearby keeping an eye on things."

"Oh my. Nature is so interesting. This would be a nice lesson for my class when school starts." The young teacher glowed with excitement.

"I understand that you're staying at the Jones Place. Will you be teaching classes there? In the ranch house?"

"There's a side building, a bunkhouse. Mr. Hawkins is having the place fixed up as a classroom. This is all so exciting." Miss Williams's eyes darted around the open area. Apparently, the pups had moved on to new adventures because the bird was no longer making ruckus.

The Sheriff smiled inwardly, thinking about the young lady in front of him, so fresh and innocent, and in a way, so vulnerable to the rigors and rough life on the Texas prairie. He thought of his own life, at fifteen working on a ranch doing the work of men, a soldier in the war of independence from Mexico, then working as a Texas Ranger. On the prairie in those days, you became a man quickly, doing men's things like tending cattle, soldiering, drinking, and ranching or farming. In those formative years there were few women in the west.

To be sure, he had on occasion met a few women, but there was no one special until he had met Sarah, during his later Rangering years. Sarah was special. He had courted Sarah and they had married. And because of the dangers of Rangering, Sarah had wanted him to give up the life of chasing Indians and outlaws and start their new life together on a spread of their own. But it had ended so quickly, so tragically.

They were riding back now towards the Jones place. Miss Williams was talking, to herself it seemed, planning ideas for lessons for the children of Bent Creek, incorporating stories of life on the plains along with the standard curriculum of reading, writing, numbers, and the social studies of American government. Watching this beautiful young lady, seeing life through the eyes of the young, the adventure and excitement of new experiences, Clay Holland suddenly felt old, and tired. He and Sarah never had the opportunity to start a family of their own. Had life passed him by?

Chapter 10

Outside, an explosion caused the building to shake.

A late afternoon cool breeze now blew from the northwest foretelling a. change in the weather. The western sun glowed a brilliant yellow like a river-washed nugget of gold peering through slate-gray clouds that began to break apart offering hope that that three-week heat spell had been broken. The skies had threatened all day, with distant rumbles of thunder but the storms had bypassed Bent Creek.

All was quiet at the Cattleman's Saloon as Sheriff Holland walked up the street towards the Red-eye for dinner. Inside, it seemed as though spirits had lifted along with the relief from the heavy weather. Women were chatting with new school teacher Clara Williams. The pretty young woman had settled in and had been working at the Bent Creek Bank during its opening festivities for the interim before school would start next month.

"My usual, Miss Maria," said the Sheriff as he sat in his customary chair and table. The dark-haired nine-year-old smiled broadly, her white teeth contrasting from her dark brown skin and black hair.

The girl was back in a flash. "Un café con whisky, señor sheriff. A coffee with whiskey, Mister Sheriff." She skipped back into the kitchen.

"Special delivery for my favorite dearest friend" Betsy Brown glowed as she set a plate with large sizzling pink steak and beans, and half a loaf of golden crust bread in front of the Sheriff. The beaming blond wore her customary red dress with swishing petticoats and low-cut front revealing a robust bosom.

"All my favorite things." Sheriff Clay Holland's eyes flashed between the attractive lady standing before him and the steaming food on the plate. Their friendship had grown over the past year after he had captured and cornered the man who had shot his wife. That man, a career criminal, had elected to fight it out and died for current and past sins. Over the ensuing twelve months, the grieving Sheriff had begun a transition becoming able to move on and accept the warm entreaties of a woman before him. "Care to join me?"

KA-BOOM!! Outside, an explosion caused the building to shake. Glass windows rattled with some breaking, and bottles behind the bar shook before falling causing the splash and tinkle of more breaking glass. A picture fell from its mounting on the wall.

Women screamed, pots and pans were heard clanging amid cries of pain from the kitchen, and men ran from the saloon into the street. The Sheriff suddenly found himself on the floor cradling Betsy in his arms, waiting for another boom. There was a moment of dead silence that followed and a light cloud of dust floated in the dining room of the Red-eye. A child's whimpering could be heard, and then outside the panicked screams of men and animals sounded surprisingly similar.

"You OK Betsy dear?" asked the Sheriff as he climbed to his feet.

Betsy stood, shakily at first, and seemed to touch her arms and legs and head, before answering. "I'm OK, at least I think so."

"Ain't no cannon in town. Building shaking like that, broken glass; sounds like the Seguin earthquake of 1847. I remember Ranger Captain Jack Hays talking of it. I've got to check for damage," he told Betsy. His eyes scanned the room and then he raised his voice to the others still in the Red-eye. "Stay here, this building looks undamaged, just some broken glass. I'm going out to check for damage."

A dark cloud rose from down the street, where the Sheriff's office sat next to the Bent Creek Stable. Windows were broken in the front of the bank and closer at McCann's Mercantile. A few men were venturing forth some dazed, others cautiously looking at the damage. In the distance was the sound of horses galloping away from town. Sensing no obvious immediate threat, the Sheriff walked towards the growing smoke ball drifting skyward shaped like a giant mushroom, holding his hand just over the Colt in case. As the smoke drifted higher, he saw that the back of the sheriff's office and jail had been blown away, a few embers continuing to burn.

"Jailbreak! They blew the back wall off the office!" The words came out as a loud exclamation, as other men edged closer to see. The Sheriff drew his Colt in case there might be gunplay be the escaping prisoner, Darrell Peterson. But the prisoner was gone. There was a smoldering straw mattress amid a pile of splintered lumber that had been the office. The metal jail bars were bent and pulled away from the damaged wall where an explosive charge had been set.

"It's a wonder anyone lived through that," said a cowboy who had approached from the Cattleman's Saloon.

The Sheriff nodded and looked around, finding footsteps and drag marks. "Tracks here. One walking, dragging something. Maybe he didn't, or maybe he had to be helped to get away." He picked up two Winchesters that had been locked in a now splintered cabinet that had once been on the wall in the office. The heavy wooden desk looked dusty but otherwise unscathed. In it, the Sheriff found several boxes of .44 ammunition and a half-empty bottle of whiskey.

There was movement next door at the back of the stable. It was Washington, leading a skittish horse into the back door of the stable. Some straw was blackened and smoking surrounded by a splash of water on the surrounding ground.

"Sheriff, suh, I should of acted faster." The hostler Washington, spoke excitedly, his movements animated, jerky. His dusty appearance suggested that the impact of the explosion had blown the man to the ground. "The animals, they told me trouble around, but I was working on a shoeing a mare, paid no attention."

131

"Are you OK, Washington?"

"Whazzat?"

"I said are you OK?" The Sheriff raised his voice as if speaking to a deaf man.

"Cain't hear ya, suh. Jest like battle, when they firing them cannons. My ears is ringing."

The Sheriff held the former Buffalo Soldier's shoulders and looked him up and down checking limbs for injury, then spoke loudly close to the old man's ears. "You look all right Washington. Your hearing should come back in a bit."

"Yessa, suh, I heard them horses complaining, that there's trouble outside. But I was fittin' a shoe." The old man was still speaking loudly, but seemed to be calming down. As a former Buffalo soldier, he had been in many Indian wars including a few where the cavalry had tried to bring cannon to bear on some Indian camps. The old soldier had proven himself on the battlefield and as an on-call deputy when the Sheriff had been injured in a shooting the year before.

"The roan, Washington, can ya saddle the roan?"

They walked quickly into the stable and saw that many of the horses were skittish. Washington spoke, his voice now softer and deeper. "Easy there, girl. It's all right." He grabbed a handful of apples from a small feedbag and offered one to each of the animals on the side of the stable closest to the wall where the explosion had occurred. The roan had been stomping and pacing anxiously in its stall, but calmed as the Sheriff and the hostler approached. "Easy, there girl, here ya go."

"Sheriff Holland, sir, if you're going after that man, that Peterson fella that shot Jonesy, I wanna be part of the posse." The voice was soft-spoken, beginning hesitantly, but in the final statement showed determination.

The Sheriff turned towards to voice at the doorway of the stable. It was Deever, the forty-year-old former ranch hand who had worked for Jonesy, now a ranch hand on the Smith Ranch. He was a humble man with a perpetual two-day growth of whiskers who always looked like he just woke up after sleeping in the same homespun clothes day in and day out. Despite his unkempt appearance, he was effective on a horse with a rope in hand handling cattle. "He done shot Jonesy, and now this. I wanna help."

"I understand your concern. And I can always use another hand. We're pulling out in a few minutes."

As Washington worked efficiently to get the blanket, saddle, and bridle on the roan, the sheriff rummaged through the rubble to collect a few belongings needed for the pursuit. Betsy Brown found her friend digging through the pile of rubble that had once been the Sheriff's sleeping room behind the jail. The force of the blast had knocked items off walls and onto the ground. Betsy brought a week's supply of food and sent Maria back to the restaurant for a coffee pot. In a few moments, with a saddlebag full of supplies and ammunition, the Sheriff and Deever were on the trail of the escaped prisoner and his accomplice. The drag marks lead down to a creek bed behind the jail. Footprints and horseshoe markings showed that horses had been tied there for a quick escape. The trail led westerly.

Chapter 11

"Two animals bearing riders headed that way."

The hot weather had returned to south Texas taking its toll on the trackers and their animals. With a strong horse and moderate conditions, a rider can generally average twenty to forty miles a day. The Sheriff's trusty roan, a veteran of long steady trail rides and pursuits, eagerly chewed up the miles consistently welcoming the high mileage exercise. But the heat takes its toll and riders tracking another must limit their riding to daytime hours when there is sufficient light to follow. Add to that fact, ranch hand Deever, who had joined in the pursuit as a deputized posse member, rode a horse from the Smith Ranch remuda where animals were part of a large herd that enjoyed a daily respite as the Smith cowboys rode a fresh horse each day. Deever's horse was showing signs of weakness after just two days on the trail, slowing the pursuit.

The trail headed northwesterly out of the subtropical regions along the lower Rio Bravo Valley, an area that is dry and covered with grasses and thorny brush, and moved into the area referred to as the hill country. In this area, the terrain becomes hilly, with many springs and steep canyons, and some hidden, underground lakes and caves. With the change in the contour of the land and the foliage, tracking became more difficult. They knew that the escaped prisoner Darrell Peterson was known to be from El Paso, but the Sheriff could not afford to assume that was the escapee's destination.

By the third day, the trail had led to a campsite in a ravine containing a small lake. Here, they encountered evidence that Peterson and his accomplice had exchanged horses. There were remnants of a campfire and hoof prints of waiting fresh animals. It was late in the day and was a good resting point with ample water and grass for the tired horses. As Deever started a fire on the ashes left by the escapee, the Sheriff scouted the area. There was evidence of another rider with three horses, and two trails leading away, with three animals heading south and two animals continuing in the northwestern direction.

"Two trails, so who do we follow?" asked Deever. A competent horseman who knew how to work cattle, Deever was learning a lawman's skills of tracking, trailing, and anticipating the actions of a fleeing outlaw.

"Two animals bearing riders headed that way," said the Sheriff pointing to the northwest. He paused to assemble the fixings for a cigarette and lit his smoke as his eyes checked the tracks on the ground. "And this other group of three animals shows one rider and two un-ridden with the tracks we been following up from Bent Creek. This means that the feller who set up this jailbreak arranged for the explosion for the escape and back-up mounts to wait here to aid their flight."

In the morning, they set out following the two horses bearing riders. It was obvious that the escapees were now moving faster towards the big bend region on fresh horses. They were headed through an area called Paisano Pass. About an hour into the day four ride, the Sheriff noticed more up and down movement of Deever's mount and shorter stride length. To the Sheriff, those actions suggested possible hindquarter lameness.

"You're bouncing around there, Deever. Your mount coming up lame?" asked the Sheriff.

"She's tough. We gotta keep moving to catch that Peterson fella."

"We'll be in the Big Bend region soon. Can't let ourselves get stranded in a desert area. It would be a death sentence," insisted the Sheriff. "Let's take a look."

On close inspection of Deever's horse, they noticed stone bruising on the sole of the hoof and a slight puffiness on the leg that indicated swelling. They rested the horses for a few minutes and then observed a distant dust cloud, suggesting the presence of a moving herd of animals. After a brief respite, they headed towards the dust cloud. Passing a stand of cottonwoods along a creek, they saw a small ranch with a couple of cowboys working a herd of cattle. As they approached, one of the cowboys rode out to meet the two approaching riders. The rancher had pulled a Winchester from the boot under his saddle.

Seeing the weapon and reading the rancher's nervousness, the Sheriff slowed his horse to a walk and held up his right hand in a peace gesture away from the Colt on his right hip. The Sheriff's brass badge on his chest glistened in the sunlight. "Howdy. I'm Sheriff Clay Holland from Bent Creek. This here's my deputy Deever."

The rancher nodded, saying nothing. His companion had taken a position off to the side, his hand on a pistol.

"We're trailing an escapee and his partner. See anybody pass by heading westerly?"

"A pair passed by near here yesterday. Looked like trouble. Thought you two might be them, back again."

"Was one of them tall? All of six foot four or more, dressed in a white shirt with a string tie and dark pants with white pinstripes held up by leather suspenders?" asked the Sheriff.

"Yep, that's him, with a wrap around his head. Claimed he was hurt from a bushwhack by some outlaws. Had a strong voice," said the rancher. "Jest looking for whiskey if you ask me. They was trouble."

"Which way did they go?"

"Northwest, over El Paso way."

"That's our man. Broke out of Bent Creek Jail, wanted for murder," said the Sheriff, as Deever's horse snorted and shuffled on three legs favoring the sore hind hoof. The men watched the horse's movement. "My deputy's animal is not bearing up well, going lame. Wondering if you'd have a spare animal we could borrow, maybe make a temporary trade. We'll get our men captured and then return your animal. Deever here works for James Smith. He's good for it."

"Smith? The Ranger? Saved my hide a few years back. Happy to oblige."

In a matter of minutes, Deever's animal was swapped out for a sorrel. The men had a quick bite to eat at the insistence of the rancher and refilled their canteens. Moments later they were back on the trail at a canter seeking to make up time tracking the escapee.

Chapter 12

The El Paso salt war...got the salt flats locked up.

In the lush fields along the hill country trail, bluestem grasses had changed to the grama bunch grasses that tolerated the drier landscape consisting of creosote, ocotillo, yucca, and prickly pear native to the southwest desert areas. Track marks showed better on the dried trail. The Sheriff nudged the roan to a canter and they began to eat the miles closing the lead. Though the landscape was drier, it was picturesque with panoramic views of wide-open spaces with rugged plateaus and desert mountains under a bluebonnet sky.

A quiet man accustomed to lonely days in the saddle, the Sheriff's mind kept busy watching the trail, eyes ever alert scanning the horizon far and then circling near watching for a sign of movement from boulders or escarpments along the trail providing cover to a sniper. The soreness in the Sheriff's leg was an ample reminder that Peterson had already bushwhacked him on their last outing. There was a partnership with the roan, his trail companion who alerted his master to possible danger from the smells of the landscape or the movement of the desert's resident creatures like the red-tailed hawk that flushed a ringtail from the security of a creosote bush into the open for a life and death race to underground cover.

The Sheriff talked to the roan from time to time acknowledging the animal's reactions along the trail. The roan's ears twitched and the animal snorted as the ringtail scurried among rocks and scrawny bushes for other cover. "A little desert excitement, huh?"

"What's that, Sheriff?" Deever thought the comment was directed to him.

"Hawk after a ringtail for dinner. You just missed the action, there Deever. Stay alert man."

"This is a long ride. How long you before you expect we'll catch him?"

"I can see that they're loafing now, not pushing as hard as before. We're gaining on 'em. Maybe by tomorrow. We're gonna have to really pay attention. This guy already bushwhacked me last time out.

The jagged mountains were now visible on the western horizon as the golden sun turned a scattering of late-day clouds to crimson. The Sheriff squinted, holding his hand to shadow his eyes from the western glare. "Up ahead, there's dust in the air, a small cloud, couple of riders. Likely our men. We gotta cover our fire tonight," said the Sheriff as he steered the roan over towards some boulders along a dry wash. "We'll make camp here. Round up some of those mesquite and creosote twigs. Put the fire up against that boulder to cover the fire from view."

As the sun dropped behind the mountains, darkness came quickly and the temperatures fell. The saddles were pulled from the horses; the animals were wiped down and picketed near some bunch grass. Deever had a fire going and the coffee on. After dinner, the two men dowsed the fire and settled into bedrolls looking up at the sparkles in the sky and the milky cloud overhead that some called the milky way.

"Makes me feel so small," observed Deever. Somewhere in the distance, a coyote howled, and moments later another answered. They heard a squeak and a fluttering of wings somewhere in the darkness. The horses remained calm. Then a quiet settled about the area.

"Wake up. Sheriff, wake up. Sa…someone's out there." Deever shuffled along the ground reaching for the Sheriff's shoulder. A short distance away, the horses snorted and stomped nervously.

The Sheriff bolted up quickly, his hand finding a Colt. He held a finger up to silence Deever as his senses came alert.

"Oh,..oh, over there," whispered Deever, a hoarseness in his voice. "A light, I saw a light moving over there, just past that ridge."

The Sheriff cocked the Colt and swung it in a large semi-circle scanning the darkness. The horses snorted again, giving a whinny that sounded more like a crying infant. The Sheriff crouched next to the boulder that had shielded their fire from the west.

There it was. A light floated some fifty yards away glowing a dull white like a lantern carried through the night. But there was no noise out there in the desert, no footsteps, no squeak of a saddle nor clink of metal spurs. Just a white round ball of light floating one way, then the next, maybe head high but moving faster than a man could walk.

Deever followed the Sheriff to the relative cover of the boulder, breathing heavily, eyes widened like eggs in a skillet. His voice came out in an anxious squawk. "What is it? I woke up and saw it, a mysterious ball of light suddenly appeared above desert foliage. For a moment it was still, then brighter, then dim, like a lantern turning on and off. Scared the crap outta me. Then I called you."

The Sheriff shook his head, eyes locked on to the floating light, the Colt following. The yellow-orange glow of the light grew with an intensity to almost blinding brilliance. Then suddenly, the ghostly light darted across the desert and disappeared. The horses quieted.

"Wha...what was that?" Deever's voice wheezed.

"I heard tell of orbs at Gettysburg. Folks tell stories lights in the night skies over the fields where soldiers died," said the Sheriff, shaking his head in disbelief. He holstered the Colt. "Some say it's spirits of the dead rising."

The night seemed to drag, with the tossing and turning in their bedrolls unable to sleep after the disturbing light show. Finally, the eastern sky began to gray as the Sheriff checked on the horses and then started a breakfast fire to fry the bacon and warm some coffee.

"Hello, the fire!" A voice called from fifty yards out. It had a familiar ring. Walking up from a deep arroyo leading his horse, it was Texas Ranger Bonner O'Toole. "Would that be my old friend Clay Holland?"

"Hey, Bonner! Good to see you, man. Just in time, coffee's hot," replied the Sheriff. What brings you out to the west Texas desert?"

"The politicians in Austin are concerned about what they're callin' the El Paso salt war. Feller name of Broward has got the salt flats locked up tighter than a drum. Bonner had walked up to the fire and now stood there shaking his head in mock disbelief. "After all them years of free for the taking Broward says that folks gotta pay his tariff to get salt." Folks fighting and dying over the feud. Governor Hubbard wants the killing to stop. Sending the Rangers to nip it in the bud."

"Broward, eh? I had words with that man. He tried to spring my prisoner. Then the prisoner, one Darrell Peterson escaped and I'm on their trail –"

"Escaped hell! Peterson had killed my former boss Jonesy. Sheriff Holland here tracked him down and had him in jail. Somebody set a bomb, blew the back off the jail." Deever had his dander up stepping into the conversation.

"Ooohh, wha....? Ouch!" Deever jumped back away from the fire, kicking embers and slapping at the smoke coming from his britches.

Bonner and the Sheriff laughed at the excited deputy. The Sheriff explained. "Peterson shot a rancher in Bent Creek, Jonesy, and made a run for it. I brought him back and the next day after I shagged Broward out of town, the jail is blown to bits an' Peterson is on the run. Looks to be headin' towards El Paso."

"Let's go kick some butt, my friend." Bonner smiled as he lit a cigarillo and tossed the match into the flames.

Chapter 13

"I'd a swore that there was a box of .44s on that back counter."

"There! That tree, that's the one," said Ronnie López as he reined the dun to the side of the road. Brothers Tommie and Bebe allowed their mounts to follow the leader. The orange sun dropping to the horizon behind the tree seemed to magnify gnarled old oak giving a sense of a multi-armed monster reaching out to clutch an unsuspecting traveler. Bebe gasped and shuddered at the image as a gust of evening breeze caused a creaking sound and movement in the branches.

"We're not stopping here, are we?" Fear was evident in Bebe's rat-like squeak. His horse stamped and snorted, reflecting the rider's anxiety. "I,…I don't like it here."

"That's the one, the marker for the road to Bent Creek. Just a couple of miles out of town" declared Ronnie.

"I hear tell that's a hanging tree," said Tommie. A voice of caution and reason, he shared his younger brother's discomfort with the morbid feeling that emanated from the place. "Across the way, there, that bunch of trees gives better cover. I bet there's a creek back in there."

"Alright, Tommie, go check it out." Ronnie admired the big old tree with its evil reputation. Its blackened bark and ugly reaching branches dominated the area, just as Ronnie dominated his brothers.

There was a whistle from back in the trees across the way. Tommie had found something and could be seen waving his hat gesturing for the others to follow. Bebe kicked his mount, anxious to be away from the tree that gave him the willies. Ronnie surveyed the area and then nudged his mount along.

"See here, Ronnie, creek over there, these cottonwoods keep us out of sight of travelers but we can see whose passing by. You picked a good area, Ronnie." Tommie knew how to give his brother credit for ideas, to make it seem like, as the older brother, Ronnie made the decisions. Ronnie had a big ego and a quick temper, thinking that his way was the only way. When they were younger, Tommie had learned the hard way, losing a tooth and getting a face full of dirt, before recognizing that his older brother was like the wolf who used force to lead the pack. Though both boys were close in stature, Ronnie was physically tougher and hit harder. Tommie recognized that his older brother was a dirty fighter with face-to-face confrontation instincts, and was now faster with a Colt.

Tommie pictured himself as the wily coyote, shrewd, conniving, seeing the bigger picture, able to anticipate problems, and plan ahead. But now he played to Ronnie's ego, using false praise to plant ideas to manipulate his older brother subtly.

Ronnie stood in the clearing barking orders. "Bebe, picket those horses, rub them down and get a fire started. Tommie and I are working on the details for this job. Tomorrow I'm going to town."

The next morning, Ronnie rode into Bent Creek, taking note of the newly constructed two-story wood frame bank on the east side of town. Ripe for plucking, he thought. Across the dusty street was a stable with a negro hostler, and next door was a burned-out building. Two laborers were picking up pieces of burnt and broken lumber, stacking salvageable items, and tossing scrap into a small fire. Further along, there was a saloon, several other small buildings, a doctor's office, a general store, and another saloon from which emanated the mouthwatering aroma of cooked meat. A few people moved about looking like Texas ranchers and cowboys, and horses were tied up at the hitches in front of the saloons. A woman was placing supplies from the general store into her wagon while a small child spun a top on the bench seat.

Nobody took notice as Ronnie tied his horse in front of the Red-eye, the saloon that smelled like steak. In his canvas pants and homespun shirt, with scuffed shoes, he looked like one of the laborers who worked at sorting the burned-out lumber down the street. Always prepared, a small pistol was hidden in a pocket of his trousers. He walked across the street where the storekeeper struggled to help the woman load the wagon with several large canvas seed bags. Unnoticed, Ronnie entered the store and circled among the stacks of merchandise, food items in one corner, women's dresses and soft goods in another corner, boots, and shoes in between, and then a section of men's shirts and trousers in another corner.

On a back counter, there was a box of .44 ammunition. Ronnie glanced about and then over his shoulder. He was alone, as the merchant groaned in his struggle to help the woman outside. Then, there was a man's voice and the clumping sound of shoes on the steps up to the boardwalk in front of the store. Ronnie squeezed through the door as the merchant came in.

"Can I help you, young man?"

"Um, no sir. I'm fine."

"Find what you're looking for? We have nearly everything needed for a homestead on the range."

"No. I'm fine." Ronnie walked along the boardwalk and around the corner. A few minutes later, Ronnie walked from between the buildings back to the street and down towards the bank. As he approached the building, he paused and looked both ways up and down the street. His eyes returned to the bank building and he scanned its size, doors and windows, and a side alley. He waited as a lady came out of the bank and down the stairs heading across the street.

Ronnie casually entered the bank, pausing just inside the doorway to look around. There was an empty desk on the side of the bank lobby situated so that it looked out over the street. Along the back wall was a chest-high counter with three glass-paned windows behind which stood two bank tellers, both men. The third teller window was empty. Two men stood at the teller windows while a woman waited in line at the second window. Behind the teller line was the vault, and a large shiny steel doorway swung open showing vault boxes inside. Next to the vault was a closed door that looked to be a private office. A sign on the door said "President." One man stepped away from the teller, his hands empty, apparently concluding his business of putting money into the bank for safekeeping.

"Hello there, young man. Are opening a bank account here?" The customer had the look of a rancher, wearing jeans, tall boots, a dusty work shirt, and a white cowboy hat.

"Uhm, just thinking about it." Ronnie decided that he didn't want to stay too long, he didn't want anybody to recognize him. Something about that cowboy, he had the look of a lawman. He turned and followed a woman out of the building, then disappeared around the corner and down a back alley behind the buildings that fronted Bent Creek's main street. He picked up a parcel he had stashed earlier and was startled by the bark of a dog, causing a nervous glance around. He turned between two buildings and was out on the street again next to the dun resting three-footed. He slipped into the saddle and nudged the dun out of town on the western trail. As he rode away, Harold McCann, proprietor of the general store stood on the boardwalk in front of the store.

"I'd a swore there was a box of .44s on that back counter, and now they're gone."

Chapter 14

Dark eyes flashed and she seemed to float, her hips swinging and swaying.

The three lawmen continued their northwestern trek into the west Texas desert. In the distance to the north, the Guadalupe mountains rose like a jagged purple saw contrasted with white puffs as clouds drifted over the serrated tops. Below on the ground in front of them, the trail of hoof marks turned onto a two-track trail.

"They've turned northward here," announced the Sheriff as he reined in the roan. He pullup up the canteen that hung from the saddle horn. He felt that nagging urge for a whiskey, but the second hidden canteen was empty. Water would have to do. He took a swig.

The other riders stopped now three abreast. The men looked up the trail leading into a white sand flat interrupted by occasional clumps of yellowed bunch grass. A mule skull lay in a dry wash just off the two-track. Overhead, the late afternoon sun beat down causing sweat under hatbands and on shirt collars. The panorama was desolate and dry, devoid of other creatures and plant life, evidence that even desert plants avoided the area.

"This is the road to the salt flats," said Bonner as he struck a match and lit his cigarillo. "So, your man is heading to the salt flats. You said he worked there, right?"

"But, what's that up there?" asked Deever. The men walked their horses up toward several large boulders which and been rolled over the hardpan two-track to block passage by wagons used to haul away the salt. Any attempt to pass around the barrier would be thwarted by wagon wheels sinking into the soft soil.

"That's Broward's handy-work. He's blocking roads in and out of the salt flats," explained Bonner. "A rider can enter, but no loaded wagon is gonna get out of the flats except on his road where he collects the tariff."

"And that's on the other side, over by San Elizario," said the Sheriff. "I say we head over that way. A man's gotta eat and drink. I figure we'll find our guy in town.

Bonner led the way, and by sundown, the three lawmen rode into the dusty town of San Elizario. It was a village really, just a collection of adobe huts surrounding a square dominated by a large chapel built of adobe bricks in the Spanish Colonial Revival style. The building was all whitewashed, with circular arched-shaped doors and windows. At its rounded top stretched a bare cross over an opening with exposed brass bells. The riders paused to watch as a white-haired peon woman slowly pulled her ancient body up the two steps holding on to a black-haired young lady who balanced her efforts between the grandmother and a toddler trailing along tugging to the long dress. The heavy door squeaked as the women struggled to pull it open and silently slip inside.

"I feel like we crossed into Mexico," said Deever as they watched the women enter the chapel.

"As a matter of fact," commented the Sheriff, "I hear tell that this little town used to be on the Mexican side, till a flood back in '29 re-routed the river to the south. Town's now in Texas."

Across the dusty roadway, the next most prominent building was a cantina, a wide flat-roofed structure with the name "Rosita's" burnt into an aging timber over the bat-wing doors. The building emanated the sounds of liquor-induced loud talk, laughter, and the pulsating sound of music.

The music had paused and then re-started as the lawmen approached the doorway. Bonner's eyes sparkled and the cigarillo glowed as he pushed his way into the dark interior. Six or eight vaqueros stood at the bar at the back and four tables spread around the room each collecting two or three drinkers. A cloud of gray smoke hung in the center of the room. The conversation paused and heads turned to check the newcomers, men with brass stars on their chests.

In the corner was a man in overalls holding what looked like a small squeeze box accordion device. The man gave three quick stomps of the foot and began moving his arms to pump the accordion, producing a quick-paced stuttering beat of the music.

"Aie-yaaa, *musica, el conjunto,*" sang Bonner as he rose his hand in the air to salute the musician. Turning to the bartender, Bonner called out above the thumping beat, "drinks for my friends."

As the bartender poured whiskey, the Sheriff scanned the darkened room lit only by candles in metal lanterns hung from each wall and mounted behind the bar. The newcomers had to squint to see through the darkness. After the bartender had refilled the glass, the Sheriff turned to his companions, speaking towards Bonner's ear. "Don't see Peterson or Broward here tonight."

"Let's wash the sand and salt from our throats," said Bonner leaning with his back to the bar while surveying the room. "It's early yet. Maybe they'll be along in a bit."

The music thumped and a dark-haired young lady appeared from a back room behind the bar. Dark eyes flashed and she seemed to float, her hips swinging and swaying about the room in tune with the beat of the accordion. She circled the room, then focused her attention on a copper-skinned vaquero playing cards at one of the tables. Her dancing circled the table, her spinning colorful skirt swishing against the young man. The card players at the table looked on in amusement while the young Mexican vaquero ignored the distraction focusing on his cards.

By now two other young ladies had entered the cantina, apparently drawn in by the music. Heads turned to note their presence and one drinker from down the bar gestured for the ladies to come his way.

The dancer continued her pursuit, swaying around the table seeking the attention of the card player, her hand now teasing his thick mop of black hair then fingers lightly tickling his mustache, her body moving suggestively. Swayed more by greed than lust, the vaquero held his focus on the cards and gold coins on the table, his free hand swatting at the dancing girl like a pesky horsefly.

The music continued shifting seamlessly to another tune. The dancer spun and twirled her way around the room now eyeing the three lawmen at the bar.

A floral perfume wafted in the breeze of her spinning movement as she passed, her flared skirt swishing the legs of the men. Bonner's cigarillo glowed between his grinning teeth while the Sheriff leaned back in mild embarrassment. Deever stood in awe and disbelief.

The dark-eyed dancer pranced away and circled back, her body gyrating invitingly towards the lawmen in synch with each thumping beat of the instrument. In a flash she had snatched the cigarillo from Bonner's mouth and in a spin, it was now clenched between her shiny white teeth, with a challenging grin. Bonner's reaction was instantaneous, his arm grabbing and pulling her towards him as in a cross-body lead, resulting in them standing face to face. He squeezed her arm tightly causing her body to stiffen and eyes to squint in resistance. Frozen in place, she glared at him. Bonner snatched back his cigarillo and then led her to the far side of the room and out the door.

The conjunto player had now taken a break and a mix of laughter with a conversational buzz in the saloon was now heard in place of the music. From outside came the sound of angry voices, one male, the other female. The words were unclear but the give and take of the suggested intensity of a two-sided dispute where neither party was backing down. Soon, inside, the hum of conversation in the saloon quieted as the drinkers sought to better hear the goings-on out on the street. Then there was a loud smack, a recognized sound of a woman's hand on a man's face.

About the saloon, men looked at one another in silent wonder and heads turned towards the men with badges pinned to their shirts. The Sheriff, accustomed to breaking up disputes between men, recognized his responsibility to take a look outside. He took two strides towards the door and paused when Bonner came strolling in hands cupped over a flaring match held close producing a cloud as his cigarillo ignited. "Well, Bonner, what was---"

"We reached an understanding," said Bonner as he took a drag on the cigarillo and pulled the dark brown stogie from his mouth blowing a gray cloud towards the center of the room. His left cheek was flushed red as a rose in the summer.

"I can see that." chuckled the Sheriff. "Do tell."

"That little hip-shaking senorita is Rosita, the proprietor. And it turns out Darrel Peterson is her man. She didn't know he was back in town. I guess she gets a little lonely for male companionship when he's away." Bonner's eyes darted about the room as he talked, keeping track of the people in the cantina. Without thinking, he touched the red welt on his cheek.

"And your understanding is…?"

"She was going to his place to look him up—"

"And warn him that the law is looking for him. A little filly shakes her tail and you turn to mush." The sheriff was already heading out the door. "Which way did she go?"

Chapter 15

...a flaming torch was shoved through the window...

The three lawmen ran across the town square in the direction Bonner had last seen Rosita walking away. For a fleeting moment, they had seen the lady who had turned a corner disappearing among a collection of small adobe houses. By the time they reached the area, there was the sound of chanting people, an angry chorus of men speaking their native Mexican tongue.

"¡Queremos sal! ¡Queremos sal!" We want salt! We want salt!

The Sheriff slowed his partners to a walk, as they approached the angry mob. The crowd was loud and fierce. There were twenty or thirty of them, mostly men, some holding flaming torches, and many holding shovels. In the darkness, a few women with small children hanging on to mamas' skirts were seen watching in the background. A leader chanted and the others repeated the chant in unison.

"¡Queremos sal! ¡Queremos sal!" We want salt! We want salt!

"Go away! Go away! No salt tonight" called out a fearful cracking voice.

Sheriff Holland worked his way around the fringe of the crowd with the torches towards the fearful voice. As a lawman and former Ranger, he had stood up to angry mobs, groups of angry people who often wanted revenge for the death of a family member or a wife or a child who had died at the hands of some miscreant who was locked up in the town jail awaiting trial and proper justice. But fired by whiskey and anger and grief, the mob had collected and demanded that the prisoner be turned over for mob justice or the jail would be burned.

"*¡Queremos sal!*" the leader chanted, and the angry crowd inched closer echoing "*¡Queremos sal!*"

"Go away! No salt tonight. Tomorrow you can have salt, those who pay the tariff will receive salt." This was a different voice, a stronger more confident voice. His baritone voice carried confidence, expecting compliance. It was a voice that sounded familiar to the Sheriff.

The man stood in front of a wooden building, on a raised platform much like the platform of a train station. He was a middle-aged man, thick and chunky, in a dark suit and vest with a small bowler hat. They had met before. This was Charles Broward, the man who had tried to buy the release of prisoner Darrell Peterson who had shot Jonesy. Standing behind Broward in the dancing shadows of the flaming torches, was Peterson, tonight, the man with the scared voice and a hand twitching just above a colt.

Off to the side, in the darkness Rosita stood watching, shivering in fear, as townspeople she knew confronted her boyfriend Peterson and his boss, the smooth-talking Charles Broward. Rosita's eyes recognized the Sheriff and his fellow lawman, but she seemed to shrink further into the shadows, fear etched in her face.

The Sheriff assessed the situation. The lawman's instincts were to quell the angry mob to prevent injury and property damage. But, more importantly, the Sheriff had made this trip to catch his fugitive who was standing just yards away with nervous fingers anxious once again to draw that Colt. First things first.

"Stop! Stop right now!" The Sheriff's voice bellowed, carrying over the crowd. He stepped towards the leader taking the torch from the man who had stirred up the crowd, throwing the flame to the ground. The man began to speak and reach for the smoking stick, but the Sheriff grabbed the man, twisting the man's arm behind his back while holding him tightly, an arm across his throat, rendering the leader helpless in front of his followers.

"Put down your shovels, put out those fires." The Sheriff's voice calmed the crowd, the murmuring stopped, and flames were lowered. "Go home to your wife, your children, to your families."

151

Seeing the crowd relent, Charles Broward spoke out once again. "Tomorrow you can have salt, those who pay the tariff will receive salt."

"Hey! Hey! We won't pay! *¡No pagaremos!*" The chants began again, the torches and shovels were raised and the crowd began pushing forward.

The Sheriff pulled the leader back, from the surging crowd. Over his shoulder, he called to Bonner and Deever, "Get Broward and Peterson inside."

Darrell Peterson drew and fired point-blank into the onslaught. Two protesters fell, and the crowds yelling and intensity grew louder, fiercer. Shovels jabbed and flames flashed as the mob continued pushing and shoving towards the salt flat operators.

Ducking and dodging the swings and jabs, the lawmen managed to pull the two salt operators and the leader into the building and bolt the doorway. The crowd yelled louder in protest. Then a stone sailed through a window crashing glass on the floor. Several other stones followed in quick succession, as the men inside tried to avoid injury from flying rocks and glass.

"Get their guns," ordered the Sheriff as Peterson and Broward were hustled inside.

"I shoulda killed you first," growled Peterson, glaring at the mob leader.

"Su novia es una puta." Your girlfriend is a whore, snarled the leader, spitting at Peterson.

"They're all dumb peons, I should charge them even more, retorted Broward.

The mob leader tried to struggle free to take a swing at Broward. Bonner and Deever were doing their best to keep the men separated.

"Tie them up. Keep 'em all separated, out of arms reach," barked the Sheriff.

Outside, there was no let-up. The intensity and noise were growing as more people in town heard the commotion and came to join in the protest. The Sheriff peaked out a window and could see the crowd growing. They began chanting again.

"¡Queremos sal! ¡Queremos sal!" We want salt! We want salt!

Then, the unthinkable happened. A flaming torch was shoved through the front window that had been broken by the thrown rocks. The flames from the torch caught one of the curtains that dangled from the now open window. Deever rushed to slap down the burning curtains. Bonner doused the burning torch. The room was now smoky and Peterson began coughing.

Then another torch flew through a side window nearly landing on Broward. Broward gasped, "For God's sake, untie us, they're trying to burn us out."

Just then, Bonner noticed tendrils of smoke seeping in from the ceiling near the back of the room. The smoke began filling the room. Broward and Peterson began coughing uncontrollably. Broward began screaming. "Get us out! Get us out. We're going to burn alive.

Sucking air and glancing around nervously, Deever cocked his Winchester and pointed the weapon out a broken window.

The Sheriff's mind was racing. This was like the Indian wars. Comanches would send flaming arrows at settlers circled wagon trains and homesteads to defend their homelands. This seemed like a never-ending night, one assault after another.

"Don't shoot, not yet. These were townspeople, with women and children on the fringe." The Sheriff pulled on Deever's shoulder, looking him in the eyes. "Wait. Not yet. We shoot back only as a last resort."

It would not be right for the lawmen to gun down fearful townspeople. For now, all they could do to minimize damage from each new attack. The neighborhood was alighted with more torches around each side of the building. They were surrounded. Was the whole town outside? There appeared to be no escape. Was this going to be like the Alamo all over again?

Outside, there was the sound of galloping horses. Then a couple of shots in the air and shouts of fear and the horses stopped in front of the doorway where moments ago the screaming mob was shoving torches through broken windows.

The riders, four, maybe more, remained mounted using their horses to disperse the crowd. The torches were dropped and people moved back quickly to avoid being trampled or kicked by a turning or rearing horse.

"Bonner O'Toole! Bonner, you in there?"

Inside, the men looked at each other, surprised, uncertain. Bonner suddenly sported a broad smile revealing shiny white teeth. He pulled a cigarillo from his pocket and lit it from one of the smoldering torches lying on the floor. He gestured to Deever to pull away the bar that secured the front door. Bonner opened the door and stepped out.

"Ranger Bonner O'Toole, reporting for duty as ordered, Captain!"

By noon the next day, Sheriff Holland and Deputy Deever were heading east out of town leading prisoner Darrell Peterson, hands tied behind his back.

Though Peterson had shot into the crowd last night, the shots had only caused flesh wounds to two of the men who were protesting the salt tariffs. Sheriff Holland had stated his case against Peterson, arguing that a murder and jail escape by blowing up a Sheriff's office trumped a couple of flesh wounds and that the fleeing fugitive should return to Bent Creek to face justice for his capital crimes. The Rangers acquiesced and had arrested local politician-land owner Charles Broward for inciting a riot. Tensions had eased in San Elizario, at least for the present.

The return trip included a stop-off at the ranch near Paisano Pass to return the borrowed horse for Deever's mount. The rancher welcomed the visitors this time with sizzling steaks, some whiskey, and plenty of water to refill the canteens. The rancher had applied some homemade poultice to help drain the sore hoof, drawing out *infection*. The animal's sore hoof had healed during the resting period. The return journey continued.

Chapter 16

Today, they were going to hit the bank in Bent Creek.

The rapid tapping continued in the tree overhead. The irritating noise had been going on for the past half hour awakening the López brothers from their sleep. Nearby, the horses snorted and stamped tugging at the picket line.

"Dammit! What is all that racket?" Bebe crawled from his bedroll and looked around up in the trees trying to locate the source of the irritating noise.

"Jest a woodpecker, looking for some breakfast," said Tommie as he put several more sticks on the fire. The flames crackled and grew as he placed a coffee pot next to a pan of beans straddled across two logs that contained the fire.

The tapping resumed as the bird attacked a dead branch in search of insects near the top of a mature oak. Tommie stabbed some chunks of meat with a skewer and laid the pointed stick into the crotch of two "Y"- shaped branches on each side of the fire. The meat would warm but the stick would not catch fire.

Ronnie walked into the camp, buttoning up his trousers. "I'm hungry. What's taking so long Tommie?"

"It's cooking, needs a few more minutes."

"Hurry it up, will you?" Ronnie was a bear when he didn't eat, even harder to get along with than his usual crabby self.

Tommy shrugged his shoulders in reply. Today was the big day. They were going to hit the bank in Bent Creek. It was obvious that the brothers were on edge, anxious about how the day would turn out. It was always like this. One time last year, Ronnie had beat up on Bebe an hour before they did a bank job causing Bebe to limp on a sprained ankle while carrying a heavy bag of money. Tommie did his best to mediate the tempers; arguing with Ronnie about when the food was ready would only cause a blow-up.

The rapping up in the tree resumed once again. "I'm gonna shoot that damn bird!" growled Bebe. As the runt who took the brunt of Ronnie's temper, Bebe took out his frustrations by kicking a dog or whipping his horse.

"No guns, idiot," barked Ronnie. He slapped the gun from Bebe's hand.

Bebe snorted like a horse, spittle, and anger erupting. His hand flew upward slapping at his older brother. Ronnie's reaction was faster, catching Bebe's wrist, grabbing and twisting the arm behind causing Bebe to spin around in pain.

"Ow, ow. You bastard!"

Ronnie jerked Bebe's arm up to the middle of his little brother's back, lifting Bebe to his tiptoes in excruciating pain.

"Ow, ow, ok, ok. I give."

"Tell me you're sorry."

"I'm sorry. I'm sorry. L…lemme go, please."

"Food's ready! Ronnie, here's your coffee, and some meat." Tommie knew that food would break up the family feud. Ronnie released Bebe's twisted arm and threw his little brother to the ground. "'Bout time."

Bebe got his food and skulked over near the horses to pout and eat. In the distance, upstream the tapping of the woodpecker resumed.

After breakfast, Ronnie told his brothers about the bank and his plan. Tommie asked a couple of questions, while Bebe continued to sulk quietly. Ronnie displayed his find, a box of .44 cartridges, which were distributed among the brothers. Guns were checked and loaded. Soon, the fire was extinguished, and the horses were saddled.

In the distance, the brothers heard the stage passing along the east-west road from San Antonio headed into Bent Creek. The brothers followed at a distance, stopping outside of town. Tommie offered to ride in and scout the street and report back.

As Tommie rode into town, he saw the stage stopped in front of the bank. Two men were struggling with a heavy trunk, hoisting it down from under the driver's seat and lugging it into the bank. One man stood on the boardwalk of the bank holding a shotgun, his eyes darting around the growing crowd of townspeople who came over to watch. Several ladies and men stood by observing the effort.

Tommie tried to watch from a distance, without being obvious. He crossed the street, resting his horse near the stable where inside a negro laborer appeared to be busy cleaning the stalls. Tommie strained to hear the comments of the townspeople. He could only hear bits and pieces, but there was excited talk, something about a gold shipment coming into the bank.

"Dang, that guy looks familiar," Tommie mumbled to himself. Tommie pulled out his tobacco sack and rolled a cigarette. He smiled as he lit a cigarette, and then casually nudged his dun back out of town.

"What took you so long?" Ronnie was getting impatient again.

Bebe had kept his distance from his older brother after their earlier tussle, choosing to stay over by a broad sycamore tree. Bebe was throwing a Bowie-style knife at the light and scaled brown-colored bark of the tree's tall straight trunk. The knife bounced away three times before Bebe was able to stick it blade first into the tree.

"You were right to send me in for a look-see."

"Oh yeh, why?" Ronnie's chest puffed up from credit being given, though unearned.

"The stage came in with a shipment of gold. A guard stood by with a shotgun while they carried the trunk into the bank. A big crowd watched the action."

"A trunk of gold, eh?"

"Yes, like you said, four o'clock, just before closing is best." Tommie glanced up at the sun and then to the shadows of the trees. "Looks like it's about two. Another couple of hours or so.

The next hour dragged on forever as the brothers waited in a copse of trees just outside of town. Several travelers had passed going east towards San Antone and a wagon with a lone driver had come by heading into town. In the meantime, Bebe was getting better at sticking the knife into the bark of the tall sycamore.

Ronnie was on his feet, pacing back and forth. "Stop throwing that knife, you idiot. They can hear that out there on the road. That's it. Its time. Let's go!"

Chapter 17

...ear-shattering shot of a Colt .44 inside the bank...

Holding their horses to a slow walk, Ronnie led the procession into town with Tommy and Bebe following.   They sidled up to a horse tie in front of the bank, casually dismounted, and wrapped the reins around the hitch.

"Like we planned," whispered Ronnie to his brothers. "Me and Bebe first. Tommie, you pull the Winchester and stand outside. Keep watch. I'll call if I need ya."

A man and woman walked out of the bank, down the steps, crossing the street. Ronnie started to enter the bank's door when suddenly a big busted woman in a swishing red dress swept by, trailed by an unseen cloud of her sweet perfume.

"Pardon me, young man. I need to get in here quickly before he closes."

Bebe stepped back, suddenly awkward, his feet stumbling as the attractive lady swished by, his face suddenly flushed. "Ma'am?"

Betsy hurried towards a teller window, and then seeing that the back office was open with its lone occupant in a dark striped suit and white shirt, she slipped through the small swinging counter door towards the office.

"Ma'am. Employees only behind the counter, please," said one of the male tellers, turning his attention away from the customer at his window.

"Harlan, I have an emergency." Betsy Brown had always given the bank owner Harlan Hawkins special treatment when he came into the Red-eye saloon, and she has supplied food-stuffs and servers for the new bank's open house. "I need some cash to pay one of my suppliers."

"Why Betsey! Where's the fire?" Harlan's grin glowed in surprise as the attractive lady hurried into his office.

BAM.

It was the ear-shattering shot of a Colt .44 inside the bank lobby, followed by the crashing tinkle of glass as the chandelier fell to the floor and shattered into a thousand pieces. Women screamed, one fainting outright and men gasped, jumping to avoid the shards.

"This is a hold-up." Ronnie bellowed as he waved the Colt in the faces of the cowering customers zeroing in on the nattily dressed bank president standing just behind the teller counter. "I want all the cash from your drawers. And we know you accepted a load of gold just today. I'm here for that, too."

Bebe knew the routine, and he was waving his gun in the faces of the tellers, gesturing that they fill the canvas bags he threw on the counter. One man standing near the door tried to run out but was met with a swinging Winchester that cracked across his forehead knocking him to the floor in the lobby.

"Now. Move it! Or the pretty lady in the red dress gets a bullet between the eyes." Ronnie was now behind the counter and his Colt was aimed at Betsy.

Betsy froze her eyes a hard glare at the dusty dark-haired funky smelling bandit waving a gun. Harlan gasped and his face turned ashen as he backed a half step behind the robust woman who now stood between him and the man with the gun.

"Don't be hiding behind no lady, Mr. Bank-man." Ronnie waved the gun, gesturing for the lady and the banker to move towards the open vault. "Get into that safe there and get us that gold.

The teller had filled the bags with money from the cash drawer and Bebe was carrying the bags in one hand while he kept his pistol pointed toward the customers. He set the bag on the desk that looked out over the street and waved his gun towards the customers huddling fearfully in the corner. He kicked a fallen hat in their direction. "Now, you people, put your valuables, cash in that hat."

They looked, too afraid to move. Emboldened, Bebe stepped forward, pointing the gun at the ashen-faced bearded old man wearing a confederate gray tunic. The man puffed up his chest and growled, "I survived Vicksburg. I ain't afraid of you."

Bebe swung his pistol, hitting the old man in the face causing him to slump at his feet. Bebe pulled a gold pocket watch from the man's belt and the other customers then began dropping valuables and cash into the hat.

In the vault, Ronnie had jammed his colt into Betsy's back and the panicky Harlan Hawkins stumbled quickly to open one of the vault drawers. Since she was fourteen years old, Betsy had learned to deal with men, to read them, figuring ways to find a man's weakness to survive, and now to thrive as the owner of the Red-eye. Sometimes, you fight, sometimes you wait for the right opportunity.

"Oh, you're hurting me, Mister uh, why I don't even know your name." Betsy leaned back slightly, allowing her hair to tickle the man's face, her perfume to capture his imagination. "So strong, so brave, I can tell---"

"Stop that!" Ronnie pulled back and away, the gun coming off the lady's back. "C'mon, get them coins," he snarled to the banker who was scooping gold coins into a canvas bag.

Tommie held his place by the door, watching Bebe and the customers inside as well as checking for activity on the street. He yelled in to Ronnie. "C'mon let's go. What's taking so long back there?"

"Gimme it. Gimme it!" Ronnie grabbed the bag of gold coins from the banker and backed out of the vault.

Betsy saw a broom propped in the corner and felt relief as the fearful sweating man moved away. This was her chance. In a fast fluid motion, she grabbed the broomstick and swung it at Ronnie causing him to rear back out of the way, his foot slipping causing him to stumble from the heavy weight of the gold in the bag. He swung the Colt, and a shot roared as he cleared the door of the vault.

Betsy grunted, stumbling from what felt like the kick of a mule, and then she fell. Harlan Hawkins emitted a squeak like a pig, freezing as events unfolded quickly. Drops of blood spurted onto the floor.

In the middle of the bank, there was a rush of movement, the clump of feet, and heavy puffs of exertion. The three men were out on the boardwalk and scuffling to mount excited horses.

"Stop, or I'll shoot." A voice called from somewhere across the street.

There was a nervous whinny of a horse, a stomping of hooves, and then a pistol shot, answered by a boom of a rifle, clicks of a lever action, and another boom. Horses raced away leaving a momentary silence.

Chapter 18

"Miss Betsy was in the bank when the robbers came in..."

It had been a long day, at the end of a long week. Shadows grew long in front of them as they trekked eastward. The horses were lathered and bone tired. Prisoner Darrell Peterson had been complaining for the last three days, refusing to shut up about saddle sores, tight rope around his wrists tied behind his back, and any other contrived ailment that came to mind. Covered in west Texas trail dust, Deever was exhausted and falling asleep in the saddle. Even Sheriff Holland, seasoned trail rider and former Ranger, admitted that his aching fifty-five years old body was not up to the rigors of the old days. It was only the instinctive leadership of the roan leading the other horses down the known path home that kept the motley trio on track after a ten-day round trip.

As the horses walked down Bent Creek's main street, a pall hung over the town. It was not the usual celebratory return like times past when the Sheriff returned to town with a captured prisoner. The Sheriff sensed the difference right away, wondering what had happened. A few people on the street had nodded to acknowledge his return but then had looked down or quickly away as if to avoid some foreboding event.

A makeshift Sheriff's office had been erected over the ruins of the old office that had been blown to bits by a bomb, the explosion that allowed prisoner Peterson to escape. The horses were reined in here, and the lawmen wearily slumped from their saddles, admiring the handy-work of the repaired office.

"Yessa, Mista Sheriff, it's good to see you back, suh." Washington looked older and tired, his curly black hair now showing signs of whitening near the ears. He took the reins of the horses and instinctively gave each animal a quick once-over with a quick eye and a floating hand identifying the ravages of a ten-day ride. The animals were rewarded with a bite of an apple and a pat on the neck.

"Howdy Washington. Good to be back." The Sheriff stretched sore muscles and rubbed at his lower back, wincing silently from touching a sore spot.

"Somebody gonna help me get down?" wined prisoner Peterson whose movement was limited by his hands tied behind his back.

Washington waved his hand up to the man to swing his leg around the saddle and then guided him to the ground. The old hostler chewed on a small gob of spruce tree resin, working it around in his mouth, and then spit a small glob into the dust next to the building. He gave the prisoner a nudge towards the Sheriff, releasing his grip only after the Sheriff had a hold of the man. "Mista Smith, he inside waiting for you, suh."

"Out chasing a mule deer, Clay? Or just lollygaggin'?" Rancher James Smith stepped out of the door, ribbing his former Ranger partner. "My riders reported you in the area early yesterday."

"Ten-day ride. Safe, not sorry. What brings you to town to welcome me back?" asked the Sheriff. The men walked back inside the newly re-constructed office, which had that fresh-cut timber smell. The old desk was in its familiar spot. "Don't suppose you refreshed my little bottom drawer stash, did you?"

Deever pulled a key from the ring dangling on the wall and led the prisoner back to the newly constructed jail area. The blacksmith must have worked overtime to rebuild a jail cell.

"Did you one better. Brought you a bottle of my special Tennessee bourbon." James smiled as he pulled a black labeled whiskey bottle from the bottom drawer. The smile on his lips did not reach the serious glint of his eyes. "You're gonna need it."

"Why? What's going on? This town has a pall about it like the day General Lee died."

James poured three glasses on the desk and nodded to the lawmen to take a drink before replying. The men took a hearty swallow following James' lead.

"Well, there was a bank robbery, made off with a big chunk of money and gold. And Miss Betsy—"

"What happened to Miss Betsy?" The Sheriff glared at his former partner for his games in disclosing bad news.

"Miss Betsy was in the bank when the robbers came in. She tried to break up the robbery, taking a whack at the robber with a broomstick, and—"

"Tell me what happened to Miss Betsy!"

"Doc's taking care of her. She took a bullet in the side, through and through. Doc says she's gonna pull through…"

The Clay Holland was already out the door, lumbering down the street to Doc's place. There had been many a day that, as Sheriff, he had spent time at Doc's questioning an injured man or some outlaw. But he had never expected that he would be there to see Betsy. His mind raced, memories flashed. There were images of Betsy's smile and humor in the restaurant, her patience and support during the difficult time after the death of his wife, and again her caring presence after he had caught and killed the man who had slain his wife.

Betsy seemed to anticipate his needs and to meet them before he even asked. Now he realized that Betsy had been an important part of his life for many years and that she had helped him to grieve and to heal. He understood that Betsy had always been a friend, and now had grown to become someone special, very special. Was this love? Clay Holland hadn't used that word in so long.

Running now, there was a sudden sense of loss, a gaping hole in his heart, a fear of what his life might be like without Betsy's smile and without her pleasant company. And yes, there was that great cooking, too. It was a feeling of pain that he hadn't felt since his wife Sarah had died. What would he do? He couldn't go through that kind of loss again. No! James had said that Betsy was going to make it. She just had to make it. He wouldn't let her die. Oh, please God. Clay acknowledged that he was not a religious man, but this day, as he ran across the town of Bent Creek, between the winded gasps, words came out of his mouth, "Oh please God, don't let her die."

Chapter 19

"...gonna get the man who did this..."

Clay Holland burst through the door at Doc's place, now gasping for air. At fifty – five, he had spent most of his life on the back of a horse or leaning up against a bar in some saloon, or sitting behind the desk in the little office provided by the town of Bent Creek. There may have been occasional fisticuffs with some disruptive drunk, but running was not a regular part of an aging sheriff's daily routine.

"Doc! Doc, how's Betsy?"

"Whoa, Clay. Quiet." Doc's response was a stage whisper. "She's resting in the back room. So many visitors coming by, I had to put her in the back bedroom while I guard the front door."

Clay leaned in to Doc to push his way to the back room, but the retired civil war medic held his ground like a stubborn bull.

"Clay? Is that you?" Betsy's voice sounded weak and tired. "It's OK, Doc. Come on back Clay."

Doc released his grip and stepped to the side letting his friend pass to the back room. Betsy lay in the bed wrapped loosely in a sheet, propped up to a semi-sitting position by an old coat rolled into a tight bundle to serve as a pillow. She smiled, as Clay charged through the door. Clay froze suddenly, dropping to one knee, his hand reaching out tentatively, touching Betsy's hand.

"I,...I was afraid..." The words ended unsaid; a tough Texas Sheriff humbled by unspoken possibilities.

"You afraid? Haa! Dusty old Ranger like you ain't afraid of nothing." Betsy laughed, but then grimaced as her mid-section shook, then let the laughter flow despite the pain. She squeezed Clay's hand. "Besides, it takes more than a misfire to knock ole Betsy Brown outta commission."

"But, I couldn't..." The unspoken fears still would not materialize into words.

"I been shot before. I bet you didn't know that, did you?" Her eyes twinkled, knowing that, momentarily, she had an upper hand with a man of strength who was now weak with emotion.

"I'm,...I'm just glad you're all right, Betsy.

There was a pause. His eyes had moistened, and Betsy waited for words, feelings still to come. Their hands each squeezed the other, their eyes meeting in a silent connection of warmth. Clay's lip quivered as if words were trying to escape. His eyes then darted down to Betsy's midsection where a blood-stained bandage was wrapped tightly.

Clay's eyes rose again and Betsy observed, the countenance of fear on the Sheriff's face now replaced instead by a steely cold determination.

"I'm gonna get the man who did this to you. I won't stop until he's in my jail or dead." The Sheriff stood and was out the door in one swift flowing movement.

Back in the Sheriff's rebuilt office, James Smith and Deever were talking when the Sheriff came barreling through the door.

"Who did this? There had to be witnesses. What did they say? Did anybody go after him?" Sore back and saddle aches forgotten; the Sheriff was ready for another man-hunt.

"Hold your horses, Clay." James Smith's former role as a Texas Ranger was evident in his calm demeanor and response to his friend and former partner's rush for retribution. He held out a glass of the Tennessee bourbon. "First things first. Sun's down, in case you haven't noticed. Impossible tracking. Wet your whistle and then we'll have a talk with banker Hawkins."

The Sheriff slugged down the glass of the smooth whiskey, nodding a thanks to James. "Let's go!" Deever, tired from the ten-day trip, elected to keep an eye on prisoner Peterson while the two former Rangers marched across the street.

The bank was closed and employees had gone home, but candles still burned as banker Harlan Hawkins worked alone in his office. The Sheriff banged on the door, and Hawkins looked up nervously and then walked towards the door nervously peering into the darkness outside.

"Hawkins! Open up. Sheriff Holland here."

The lock rattled as the banker opened the door and stepped aside as the Sheriff and James came in. "I didn't realize you had returned Sheriff. I guess you heard, we were robbed today."

"I got back just an hour ago, and I know about the robbery." The Sheriff faced off with the banker in a challenging posture, arms on his hips. "I want to know what happened, tell me how Miss Betsy got shot in your bank."

The banker blanched, stepping back. "You accusing me of something? Say what you mean!"

"What the hell happened that you allowed gunplay shooting Miss Betsy?" There had been friction between these men ever since the banker had come to town. The bullet wound on Betsy's side was like throwing a match into gunpowder.

"Clay, robbers came in shooting, announcing a robbery." James interceded recognizing the friction between the two men. "Harlan, tell the Sheriff what happened."

"Well, Miss Betsy came in just before closing. Then there's this gunshot in the lobby, knocked down my St. Louis Chandelier. There were three of them. The one, he was the leader, he took Miss Betsy hostage, sticking a gun in her back saying he'll kill her if I don't get the gold out of the vault."

"So, why didn't you just give him the gold?"

"I,...I did. Then they got in a hurry to go, and Miss Betsy, she tried to wiggle free and hit the man with a broomstick. The gun went off."

"You didn't stop it?"

"It all happened so fast. He started out of the vault, she tried to hit him with the broom and he shot. She did get a piece of him and the shot went wild. I didn't even know it hit her until I saw her sitting on the floor and blood on the floor."

"That lady's got more gumption than you do!" snarled the Sheriff. "Three men, you say? Recognize anyone? Anyone refer to another by name?"

"I never seen them before. They all looked like Mexican, but they talked American. I couldn't see faces 'cause they wore bandanas."

"Can you describe anything about their appearance?"

"Two looked kinda like brothers. But all them Mexicans got brown skin and black hair. They all look alike to me."

"Which way did they go?"

"East towards San Antone."

"Notice anything special about the horses?"

"No, I was busy inside."

"You said they were after the gold. What did they get?" asked James.

"I'm still tallying it up." The banker gestured back towards his office. "They got cash from the teller drawers, valuables from the customers, and a bag of gold coins."

"Damnation!" James' fist hit the top of a desk in anger. "I knew we shoulda had more guards."

The Sheriff caught the glance between the two men, an unspoken judgment by his former Ranger partner who had become a prominent rancher with an apparent financial interest in the success of the bank.

The Sheriff and his former partner walked back across the street, each in quiet thought about the pursuit tomorrow.

"Clay, I'll have some men ready to join the posse first thing in the morning." The Smith Ranch had a large crew of cowboys and could spare a few men.

"You gonna join the hunt? Sounds like you got a stake in this?"

"Huh? No. I've got some business to tend to," replied James.

"Sounds like you got a stake in this," repeated the Sheriff, watching his friend's reaction out of the corner of his eye.

"Well, yes. I've made deposits in the bank,… for the security. I don't want to have too much cash out at the ranch. What are you suggesting?"

"James, you know I don't beat around the bush. I just want all the cards on the table, is all."

Later that night, while the townspeople of Bent Creek slept and the coyotes howled out on the plains, the glow of a lantern was seen in front of the bank. The Sheriff and Washington we examining footprints and hoof prints on the dusty road in front of the bank and the trail eastward.

Chapter 20

"I been shot...it's burning like a branding iron."

The López brothers pushed their horses hard for two hours until the light ran out making it difficult to see the ruts and rocks on the dirt trails that could cripple a good animal. By the time Ronnie decided to slow to a walk, stars filled the skies and a distant coyote could be heard. Tommie turned, looking over his shoulder for little brother Bebe.

"Where's Bebe? You wasn't watching, Tommie?" Ronnie was quick to assign blame.

"I was keeping up with you, Ronnie, and hanging on to this heavy bag of gold coins."

"You know you gotta watch him. Go find him."

Tommy turned his mount around and nudged the animal northward. In the darkness ahead, there was a crying sound, like a cat proclaiming its territory. Tommie drew his colt and reined in the bay. The sound seemed closer, now, more of a high-pitched squeal, like that of a hurt animal. He squinted into the darkness looking for signs of movement. The bay twitched its ears and nickered. Up ahead, there was a movement from around a bend in the road. The squeal again, and the bay sputtered, receiving a sputter in reply.

"Tommie? Izzat you?" The voice was Bebe's but it sounded like he did as a child years ago coming home hurt one day with a bloodied knee.

"Bebe? What happened? What's the matter?"

"Tommie, oh. It hurts. I,…I can't hold on anymore." There was a clink as the canvas bag that he held dropped to the ground. The horse stopped, and Bebe hunched over clinging to the animal's mane.

Tommie's bay came alongside. Tommie reached out to his little brother. "Bebe, what's the matter?"

"Oh, it hurts. I been shot. I didn't feel it at first, but now it's burning like a branding iron."

Tommie now could see the shininess of blood on his brother's right shoulder. "Hold on, Bebe. We'll take a look."

Bebe cried out again as Tommie removed the shirt to examine the wound. Bebe then squealed that cat cry when Tommie wiped blood from the shredded deltoid muscle and then bound it up tight with sleeves cut from the bloody shirt.

"Shuddup you idiot!" Ronnie screamed in a stage whisper as he came out of the darkness looming over his brothers.

"It's a flesh wound. I bound it up tight, stopping the bleeding," replied Tommie. "He needs to rest though."

"I found a campsite by a little creek, over here. Keep him quiet, will ya?" Ronnie grabbed the fallen bag containing the valuables taken from the bank customers.

"I'm thirsty," wined Bebe.

"Sshh, sshh. Sit over here, I'll get you a drink from the river." Tommie led his brother to an old cottonwood that leaned over the creek.

"No fire tonight. They'll see it a mile away." Ronnie was angry and antsy when they were on the run. "Just water and hard-tack. And no more whining like a baby, Bebe. Keep him quiet, Tommie. I got first watch."

Chapter 21

"I'm ramrodding this posse. My word goes, ya hear?"

"Well, isn't this a switch? You bringing me breakfast." Betsy's grin spread from ear to ear. "And I haven't had a chance to get all dolled up."

"You look just fine to me," replied the Sheriff, unable to control the reddening of his cheeks as he set a tray of steaming steak and eggs on a side table. "You've brought many a dinner down to my office. This just seemed like the thing, to do. Besides, the ladies over at the Red-eye had it all ready."

"Why, thank you, kind sir." Betsy tipped her head in a mock gracious bow. "How are you feeling today?"

"Still sore, but Doc says that I'm on the mend. I can't wait to get out of this bed and back to work at the Red-eye." Betsy eyed the Sheriff up and down, her expression now serious. "You look like you're dressed for war."

The Sheriff had on a double holster with a Colt on each hip and a bandolier of .44-40 rifle ammunition angled around his chest. His countenance now matched his armament. "Yes, ma'am. Posse's heading out in a few minutes. I'm gonna get the men who done this to you."

With that, he tipped his hat and was out the door. Betsy's "be careful" admonition was lost in the commotion of street noise as three cowboys rode into town. Townspeople stood by in small cliques watching and talking as if the men were going off to the battle of Bull Run.

The three riders stopped in front of the bank where James Smith was talking to banker Hawkins. It was Buck Carroll, foreman of the Smith Ranch, and two cowboys who wore Colts slung low on the hip. The Sheriff approached them, warily taking measure of the two new faces. The men looked more like gunslingers than cowhands.

"James, Buck, g'morning." The Sheriff gave a curt nod to banker Hawkins. He turned to the riders. "Ready to roll?"

"This here's Laredo Kid, that's Curt Cousins, new hands," said James as he pointed to each. "Gentlemen, meet my former Ranger partner, now Bent Creek Sheriff, Clay Holland."

From their saddles, the men nodded in acknowledgment to the Sheriff, and then their eyes turned towards James and Buck as if awaiting further direction. A lawman reads people and recognizes that facial expressions and unspoken glances carry strong meanings and reveal loyalties. This wouldn't be like other posses where inexperienced townspeople or cowhands look to the Sheriff for leadership. There was an agenda here, backed up by paid guns under the direction of ramrod Buck Carroll.

While it was good to have some additional riders in a posse pursuing three bank robbers including a leader who had shot a woman in the course of the crime, Sheriff Holland recognized that he would have his hands full matching wits with the outlaws as well as managing the conduct of the posse. But, as a former Ranger who worked under the motto "One riot, one Ranger," the Sheriff was experienced in dealing with tense situations, emotional people, and overwhelming odds.

"This is my show. I'm ramrodding this posse. My word goes, ya hear?"

From the corner of his eye, the Sheriff noticed a subtle nod from James Smith, and then the two fast-gun cowhands replied. "Yes sir." "Yes sir, Sheriff."

"I'll back your play, Sheriff," said Buck Carroll.

Hostler Washington walked up, leading the Sheriff's roan. He was followed by Tomas, a young Mexican orphan who was now helping around the stable in return for room and board. Tomas was leading a packhorse.

"Yessa Mista Sheriff. The roan, she ready to go," said Washington. He handed the reins to the Sheriff and offered a wedge of apple to the horse.

"Winchester in the boot, canteen's full, and saddlebag full of ammo. Second canteen filled if you need it. Them nice ladies from the Red-eye fixed up some sammiches and some grub for the trail. Tomas here has a packhorse with the food, ammo, and trail supplies.

"Thank you, Washington," said the Sheriff as he swung his right leg up over the saddle and settled in.

"Fer your deputies," said Washington as he handed over three badges.

The Sheriff nodded. "Gentlemen, raise your right hand. I need to deputize you." The Smith riders each raised a hand. "I hereby deputize you to enforce the laws of the State of Texas and to apprehend the bandits who robbed the Bent Creek Bank."

The Sheriff then touched the saddlebag feeling for the second canteen. The old soldier had filled it with whiskey. He turned to the Negro hostler and occasional deputy. "Your time in the cavalry shows, you know how to pack for a trail ride."

"Yessa Mista Sheriff. You all be safe now, ya hear?"

"Gentlemen! See these tracks over here?" called the Sheriff to his posse as he pointed to the ground. "These three here, these are the tracks were following, this way."

James Smith gave a wave to Buck and the others as they headed east out of town. Several townspeople standing on the boardwalk in front of the bank began to applaud as the departing posse.

In the blur of by-standers, one person caught the eye of Clay Holland. Clara Williams stood on the porch in front of the bank with a white hanky in hand, radiant in a ray of the morning sun, her hair aglow, her moistened worried eyes watching him leave.

Their eyes met momentarily. He could read her lips saying "Be careful Clay." And for those few seconds, she was the only person waving goodbye with that white hanky.

The bump of the horses brought the Sheriff back to the task at hand. He nudged the roan and set the pace at a mile-eating canter. The tracks showed that the robbers had pushed their horses, staying on the east-west road to San Antonio, and then, near the tree now called the hanging oak, the robbers had turned south still sticking to the roadway. After a few miles, they had slowed, but there was no evidence that they had stopped for the night. There were few words spoken as the posse followed the trail. By mid-day, the Sheriff stopped at a creek to rest and water the animals. Trail signs showed that the robbers had taken a break there as well, but had not camped or built a fire. As the animals drank, there was some quiet conversation among the Smith riders.

After a bit, Buck approached the Sheriff. "Sheriff, the Kid, here, he thinks that the fellers we're tracking may be fellers from down Laredo way."

"Oh yeh? Why's that?"

"Well, we were talking, Mr. Smith was telling me about the robbers, three Mexican lookin' fellers, might be brothers. The kid says that there was some scum around Laredo, a bunch of brothers always looking for trouble. They was breeds, half Mexican, half 'merican. Might just be them."

"So, who are these guys?"

"Kid thinks it might just be the López brothers. Ne'er do-well scum always in trouble, grew up on the streets of Laredo. Was always stealing anything they could get their hands on."

"Lot of Mexican blood in the area." The Sheriff lit a cigarette, blew a gray cloud, and glanced over his shoulder looking at the two fast-gun cowboys. "What makes him think these guys are the ones from Laredo?"

"Well, the banker feller told Mr. Smith that one of the robbers was a youngin, kinda slow, you know, one they call Bebe."

"I talked to Hawkins. He never told me about this."

"I guess he heard people talking after the robbery, about how the young robber still had peach fuzz, you know. He was the one who took the customer's belongings."

"So, do these brothers have a name?"

"Yep. The López brothers."

Chapter 22

"You got a beef, Kid? Make your play."

By mid-day, the posse had reached the Nueces river. The trail led to a rocky ford. The group stopped to stretch their legs, get a drink, and let the animals suck at the flowing water. During the break, the Sheriff found tracks showing where the López brothers had camped the night before.

"Camped under the trees, no fire. One of 'em's hurt. Found a bloodied shirt sleeve. It'll show them down some," commented the Sheriff as the others refilled their canteens.

"I heard your man Washington say he thought he mighta got a piece of one," replied Buck.

The Sheriff nodded. "Should make it easier to catch them. No loyalty with bandits. They'd leave a dying one if he was slowing them down."

"Don't underestimate them," said the Laredo Kid as he assembled the makings. He lit a match from his jeans and brought a cigarette to life, blowing a smoke ring in the breezeless air. "Them López brothers was scrappy urchins, street-tough. Stir up trouble with a drunk going home at the end of a night of drinking or whoring. One would distract him, and another would knock him on the head, and the third would clean out his pockets and take a gun, belt, and anything else of value."

"Sounds like you might a had a late-night run-in with these Laredo fellers," chuckled the Sheriff.

"Me? Hell no!" bristled the Kid. "Heard stories, though."

"Umm-hmm," nodded the Sheriff as he swung into the saddle and nudged his mount into the softly flowing water. First one over the river, he pulled a quick draw from his emergency canteen that had been packed by hostler Washington.

The two-track road meandered towards the south and a bit easterly through an area of grasses and thorny brush. The Sheriff watched the tracks and nudged the roan to a trot and then scanned the horizon for bushwhacking sites. The riders were lost in their thoughts. Overhead, a hawk tracked the riders circling lazily overhead for an hour before drifting back to the west. The sun tracked high, raising temperatures and stickiness of the air, until puffy white clouds gathered mid-day, breaking the sun's heat, but not the humidity. Beads of sweat trickled from hats and collars.

The roadway passed through a saddle between some rolling hills. The Sheriff raised his hand as if signaling a cavalry column to stop. "Let's take a break here. Give the horses some water. I'm gonna take a look-see from the top of this hill."

There was no argument from the others as the Sheriff nudged the roan to the rolling top of the mound. A jackrabbit was startled from a clump of bunch grass and scampered away in a "Z" route, probably heading towards its den. The roan took the flash of movement in stride, while the Sheriff watched the animal until it scurried out of sight. At the peak of the hill, he reined in the roan and slowly scanned the southern horizon, alert for movement. Some miles ahead the trail topped another ridge and there, movement caught his eye. Squinting, he stayed frozen as did the roan. A tiny speck disappeared and a dust cloud remained.

"That's gotta be them. Still a half-day out. We better pick up the pace." The roan snorted and shook its head in reply. He took another swig from the emergency canteen. With a nudge of the knees and tug of the reins, the roan turned and walked down the hill following a drainage hollow around the hill to keep his profile from view. With this move, he would approach the posse from the rear.

As the posse riders came into view some hundred yards ahead, the movements of the three men revealed an animated discussion, clearly a difference of opinion. The Sheriff held his distant position for a few minutes waiting to see how the discussion would play out. Due to the westerly breeze, the voices did not carry but it was obvious that the Kid's pointed finger to the chest of Buck Carroll who stood resolutely with hands on his hips, showing the high intensity of the discussion. The Sheriff clicked to the roan and approached.

"—didn't join this outfit to sit on my hands!"

"You got a beef, Kid?" The Sheriff wasn't about to tolerate insubordination when leading a posse.

"What's with this dawdling? You holding back? Lost your nerve?" The Kid was known for his hot temper and his fast gun.

"You want to test me? Make your play!" His hand hovered over the Colt; The Sheriff glared at the hot-headed upstart.

Surprised by the challenge, the Kid swallowed but found a dry mouth. Now facing a hard glare from a man ready to draw, the Kid realized that he had lost an offensive edge. Always before, he had backed others into a corner, having the advantage, an edge that was now lost by the Sheriff's immediate confrontation. Clay's eyes and his posture showed no fear. He was a man willing to kill if need be, even a member of the posse.

"What's with the dawdling?" the Kid repeated, without the sharp edge. "I was hired…Uhm, I volunteered to ride this posse to get these guys."

"Whatever you were hired for is between you and Smith. You take my lead on this posse or you turn in that badge. Get it?"

"Yep." The temper had simmered. A man who lived by the gun and survived did so because he learned that you chose your battles carefully.

"They're half a day's ride from here. I watched them ride over the ridge up ahead. Let's go!"

Chapter 23

"He's bleeding again. Let me tighten that bandage."

"I can't do it anymore. I gotta rest." Bebe had been lagging behind brothers Ronnie and Tommie.

"C'mon Bebe. Keep up. You can do it." Tommie tried to be encouraging.

"Leave him!" barked Ronnie, a sneer on his face. "There's a tail back there. Outta range, but they're gaining. We gotta push harder. That cry-baby is slowing us down."

"They probably know where we're heading anyway," commented Tommie as he offered a canteen to his little brother.

"I can't go on. Just a few minutes, puleese."

It wasn't that Bebe's horse couldn't keep up with the others, rather it was the bullet wound to his shoulder that caused a burning searing pain greater than any the fifteen-year-old Bebe had ever experienced. The right arm now hung useless, and it was all Bebe could do to stay in the bouncing saddle of a trotting horse. His shirt was stained in blood, from a wound that continues to leak. At night, he cried himself to sleep, only to wake with a start when he rolled over onto the wounded shoulder. Tommie had been carrying a canvas bag that Bebe had filled with the stolen belongings from the customers in the bank.

"Leave him! Or I'll put him out of his misery like a lame horse!" Ronnie had twisted in his saddle turning back, pointing his Colt towards Bebe's chest.

"Don't Ronnie." Tommie moved in between his two brothers. This wasn't the first time that he had interceded on behalf of the little one. Tommie glanced around as if looking for an escape path.

"Puleese," moaned Bebe, slumping in the saddle, now hanging on the mane of his horse.

"He's bleeding again, Ronnie. Let me tighten that bandage." Tommie said as he pulled a bandana from his neck.

Bebe was slipping lower, losing his grip on the mane, the one arm draped around the horse's withers, then rolling out of the saddle, thumping onto the ground. The horse snorted and stepped away from the bloodied young man.

"Bebe. Bebe. Stay with me." Tommie was down on his knees in the roadway shaking his little brother.

"Dadgummit! We gotta go!" Ronnie's bay was dancing in a circle, reflecting his rider's anxiety.

"He lost a lotta blood, passed out. I'll get him," said Tommie as he looked up at Ronnie.

"I oughtta shoot ya both!" Ronnie's temper boiled over again.

"So, you wanta bushwhack me and Bebe, Ronnie? Or them?" Tommie was trying desperately to re-direct his older brother's thinking.

"Huh? What?"

"You said they're following, but outta range. What about this idea?"

Tommie described his idea, repeating some of Ronnie's remarks so that it sounded like the idea was actually Ronnie's idea. Ronnie stood taller, nodding in agreement, finally saying, "Well, do it then! I gotta see where they are."

Chapter 24

"You said you know the López brothers. Tell me about them."

The Sheriff led off at a canter intending to close the gap. Before too long, they would be approaching Laredo, the stomping grounds for this outlaw band of brothers. They would know roadways and the back ways, the people and the places, the hot spots, and the hiding spots. After a few miles, he eased back on the reins and let the roan set the pace. The Sheriff's eyes continually scanned the horizon checking ahead left and right, and then close-by, left and right. It had become instinct. He was always alert for movement, a glint or reflection, any sign of the unusual, or something out of place.

After a bit, the roan had set her own pace. Over a distant ridge, a mule deer buck led a doe and a fawn up to higher territory and around a hill. On another day and time thought the Sheriff, he might have made chase. The idea of a venison steak made his mouth water. Instead, he reached into the saddlebag with the emergency canteen. A swallow warmed his throat.

He thought again about the López brothers and the fact that one of them had shot Betsy. Anger surged once again, but he pushed the urge aside. He turned in the saddle and called back,

"Hey, Kid. Need your advice on something."

A few yards back, the Smith riders had bunched together following the Sheriff. The Laredo Kid looked up, surprised.

The Sheriff wiggled a "come here" with his finger and a nod of the head. The Laredo Kid glanced at his two partners and then clicked his mount to catch up to the Sheriff.

"You said you know the López brothers. Tell me about them."

"Huh? What do you want to know?"

"You're from the same town. Your paths have crossed before. Tell me about them, what they do, how they behave, what they think. I want to know what we're facing."

"Well, there's the three of them. Ronnie is the oldest, he's the leader. Second is Tommie. They look a lot alike. The third one is named Junior, but they call him Bebe. Just a kid, still got a baby face, nary a whisker.

"So, Ronnie likely planned this job, called the shots?"

"Reckon so."

"And which one shot Betsy?"

"Cain't say for sure. Did you talk to the banker? What did he say?"

"Said they looked alike; He didn't recall anyone referenced by name." There was a momentary silence as the riders watched a hawk circle overhead gliding on the updrafts. "So, you didn't have any run-ins with them but heard stories. Any stories come to mind? Any stories that would give a sense of what we're facing here?"

"Ronnie's the hothead. Quick temper, flies off the handle at the drop of a hat. Uh, the second brother, Tommie, he's more level-headed. And the youngin', he just kinda tags along."

They rode in quiet for a few more minutes. Overhead, a few puffy white clouds scudded by in the breeze. The Sheriff spoke again. "So, Ronnie, you and he never crossed paths? Laredo ain't that big"

The Laredo Kid's lips twitched ever so slightly. He glanced back to the other two Smith riders and then scanned the horizon.

"Ronnie, he never tested you?" The Sheriff pressed.

The Laredo Kid looked ahead, unfocused, and then his eyes drifted up to the left. "One time, coming out of a saloon late at night."

"And?"

"And, he come around a corner, bumped into me. All buzzed up he was, tried to start something."

"And you? You buzzed up too?"

"No. I watch my back. Ronnie, he is a sloppy drunk, blowing off some steam. Thought he could beat me. But the other one, Tommie, he stepped in the middle and pushed Ronnie back around the corner. Saved his brother that night."

"Anything else?"

"Naw. They stayed clear of me after that."

The lawmen rode for a while in silence. The Sheriff chatted briefly with Buck Carroll. But the Smith Ranch foreman became evasive when the Sheriff tried to steer the conversation into any business activities involving James Smith or the Smith Ranch. The Sheriff felt that there was a widening gulf between him and his former Ranger Partner James Smith since Smith's ranch had grown and his perspective had shifted to ranching and business issues. And of course, Smith employees were loyal to their boss.

A mile or so ahead, a pair of turkey vultures circled. Every cowboy recognized that sign, the sign of death on the prairie. They slowed to a walk, approaching cautiously looking around for any signs of the López's.

"We saw evidence, one was shot. Maybe he didn't make it," commented Buck.

"Would they just leave a brother to rot on the prairie?" asked the Sheriff.

"Ronnie would," said the Kid.

"Keep alert," said the Sheriff as he pulled the Winchester from its boot

As the riders neared, a third black bird soared overhead. Off to the side of the road, there appeared to be a dark lump. Was it man or beast? At this distance, some several hundred yards away, it was hard to tell. The carcass, whatever it was, lay among clumps of dried grama grass, yucca, and low-growing thorny vegetation.

Closer they moved, now a hundred yards away. There appeared to be a hat, and boots at each end with a dark lump in between. Was it a blanket? Or was it a body darkened by dried blood? It had attracted the buzzards, scavengers who showed up signs of impending or recent death.

The body, or whatever it was lay near the side of the road, as an arroyo sloped away. The roadway here curved towards a saddle between two low hills and some occasional boulders were scattered about as if dropped by the Gods overhead.

Now at fifty yards, the roan twitched its ears and sputtered its distaste about the presence of death. The Sheriff signaled that they spread out, approaching at a wary walk. He then dismounted and crouched as he closed the final twenty yards.

The breeze blew lightly from the west. A dark shadow from a bird in the sky flashed by on the ground, and a horse whinnied nervously.

Bam-Bam-Bam

The Sheriff's hat flew from his head. A horse squealed in pain and reared up dumping Buck onto a yucca, where he yelled and rolled away. The chestnut carrying Curt Cousins bolted away as Cousins fell to the ground. The Laredo Kid yanked his horse away down the arroyo looking for an escape out of range. It was clearly rifle fire, apparently coming from the hills on each side of the trail.

The three men huddled behind bunches of grass, finding the lowest hollows in the ground. The Sheriff peeked around the bunchgrass that gave only minimal cover. More rifle fire buzzed overhead. Somewhere behind, the hooves of the Kid's horse could be heard. The Sheriff watched as a breeze blew the dark blanket that had covered the body, revealing two butchered prairie dogs lying between an old pair of boots and hat. From a distance, it had looked like a body. Instead, it had been a trap.

The lawmen lay flat, unable to get a clear fix on where the shots were coming from. The shooters were well hidden and not revealing themselves. Curt Cousins lay still, his horse had trailed away from the gunfire. The Sheriff could see the Buck hunched over behind a bunch of grama grass that gave visual cover but no real protection from bullets.

"Buck? You all right?" called the Sheriff.

Buck rolled over, winced, and answered. "Got a dang cactus thorn in my ass. Other than that, I'll live."

"Curt? You all right?" The Sheriff called out to the other downed rider. There was no answer. "Curt? You hit? Give me a sign."

"I'll skooch over," said Buck as he started to move towards the Curt.

A shot kicked up some dust nearby, causing Buck to roll back behind the grass. A second shot threw dust into his face causing him to flinch.

"Where'd the Kid go?" asked the Sheriff.

"Finding a spot to cover our escape," said Buck. "At least, I hope so."

184

"Scooch straight back, Right now! Into the arroyo behind you. They've got a fix on your position," called the Sheriff. The Sheriff threw a shot in the direction of the hill where he had seen a flash. He then began to push back from his position towards the dip in the ground to the rear.   As he began to slide feet first down the decline, a bullet made a dust cloud right where he had been hiding moments before.

Chapter 25

...bushwhack idea...put the lawmen in the line of fire for easy pickings.

"I got one!" called Ronnie as he cocked the lever-action and put another shot towards the men rolling on the ground near the dead dummy by the side of the road. "Hot damn!"

"You shot the horse, you idiot," said Tommie mumbling to himself from across the roadway hidden behind a boulder. And one of them looked like the Laredo Kid, he thought. He knew his shot had scored causing one man to fall. The first shot though, had sent a man's hat flying, the man on foot coming up to check on the dummy. At least they were pinned down, but one on horseback had got away. He didn't realize that there were four of them until they came around the bend and approached the ruse. It had looked so real from a distance with the hat and boots. And the dead animals had attracted the vultures so quickly, giving a realistic effect. It's amazing how quickly those vultures show up at the smell of death.

The López brothers were well hidden on each side of the road and had a cross-field of fire which gave them an added advantage. Ronnie kept popping off shots with any movement, keeping the targets pinned down, but only one lawman was clearly hit. The others were scooting around in the dirt, and one on horseback had escaped down the arroyo. Tommie looked for the escaped rider but now could not find him. When he set up the dummy and selected the spot, the arroyo didn't look so deep that it would provide any real cover. But with the movement out there, it looked like the lawmen were sneaking away under cover of the arroyo. Behind the boulder he used as cover, he heard Bebe moaning again. The baby brother just didn't have the stamina to carry his weight in an operation like this there they needed all-hands-on-deck with a weapon.

Tommie was now having second thoughts about this bushwhack idea. But Ronnie had been getting anxious, mad at Bebe, threatening to shoot his own brother who already had been hit by a bullet while fleeing the bank job. The bushwhack idea had seemed like such a great idea; create a ruse to put the lawmen in the line of fire for easy pickings, but now, they were escaping down the arroyo. And they ain't just gonna go away. No, he realized now, they'll keep coming even harder.

From his flanking position, Tommie could only see one lawman down not moving. He heard a whistle, and then in the distance saw a roan horse trotting along the arroyo followed by another horse. Could they all have escaped by disappearing down the arroyo back to find cover?

Now the shooting had stopped. Apparently, Ronnie didn't see any targets to shoot at. Tommie needed to signal Ronnie. They needed a backup plan now, an escape plan. And Bebe, he needed to get Bebe out of there, but Bebe was so weak that he could barely stay on a horse. Bebe had a bit of a rest now, and so had the horses. Maybe they could make a break for it. The horses were tethered back behind the hill. He could get Bebe mounted and make a break for it. But Ronnie was on the other side of the road, across a field of fire if the lawmen were still out there, still watching. And, he just now discovered, Ronnie had kept the gold.

It was quiet. There was no movement. The vulture had landed by the dead prairie dog and began walking towards its next meal. If the bird had landed by the corpse, that meant that the lawmen had pulled back.

Ronnie was peeking out from his hiding place looking for the lawmen, looking for a target. Tommie waved to get Ronnie's attention. Tommie pointed out toward the vulture and shrugged his shoulders. Ronnie pointed to the horses and Bebe, then waved his hands and fingers to show a running movement, pointing southward towards Laredo. Tommie nodded "OK" and then waved a "back up" movement to Ronnie, pointing to his older brother to watch the field of fire while he brings the horses for the escape run.

Tommie peeked around his boulder, again seeing only the vulture pecking at the dead prairie dog and the body of the lawman he had shot. The coast seemed clear. So, he crawled away from his hiding spot back towards where the horses were tethered. His mind was racing, figuring out how he was going to get Bebe onto a horse, ride his own mount while leading Ronnie's animal, and then race across the roadway towards where Ronnie was hiding with the gold.

When he rounded the curve of the hill, Bebe was gone. "Bebe? Where are you?" Tommie kept his voice to a loud whisper. He looked all over, there was matted grass where Bebe had been laying on a blanket, under a copse of cottonwoods. But his brother and the blanket were gone. Could Bebe have been so scared by the shooting that he ran away?

And the horses! Where were the horses? "Bebe! Where are you? What did you do with the horses?" His voice was louder, fearful, as his eyes frantically darted around looking for the animals that should be tied there.

Chapter 26

"Laredo Kid just made off with the gold."

"You looking for a way out?" A dusty man whose face was darkened with a two-day growth of whiskers and a Colt in hand stood smiling behind Ronnie.

Ronnie looked up startled by the man standing behind him. He spun his Winchester around, but the man's Colt clicked as the hammer was pulled back.

"Wouldn't do that if I was you."

The voice sounded so familiar to Ronnie. And then it came to him. This was the Laredo Kid from around town. He knew the Kid was fast and already had the drop on him. Where did he come from? Then he saw the badge on the Kid's chest. He was one of the lawmen who had been chasing them, the one who had escaped when the shooting started. And when they were shooting, he somehow got around and had flanked their position. Ronnie lowered the rifle. He hoped that Tommie was watching and would be shooting real soon and they'd escape.

"What do you want?"

"Them bags there at your feet."

"We can work out a split."

"Split, my ass. Time's a-wastin'. I'm taking those two bags, Now!"

"Now Kid, you know me from around town. You gonna need my gun to get outta this mess." Ronnie was still trying to work a deal. He didn't want to give up the gold.

"Shuddup!"

The barrel of the Colt came down in a flash across Ronnie's face, knocking him out cold. The Kid could see Tommie across the way looking in vain for Bebe and the horses. He holstered the pistol, reached down, and grabbed the two canvas bags at the feet of the now unconscious bank robber. They were much heavier than he realized. The kid stuffed the bags into each side of a large saddlebag and with a grunt hoisted it to his shoulder. In three steps he had the saddlebag over his mount and was swinging his leg over the saddle. The horse sputtered in complaint. A kick in the ribs and the animal was galloping away south towards Laredo.

On the other side of the road, Tommie heard the sound of fast hooves and glanced over his shoulder. Behind a cloud of dust, a rider was pushing his animal hard heading to the south. He wondered if brother Ronnie was making a get-away with the gold while he was still looking for Bebe and the horses.

"You lose something?" A dusty well-worn man with a sun wrinkled face walked out of the trees with a Colt in his hand, a hard smile on his lips, and a badge on his chest.

Tommie set down his Winchester and raised his hands.

"Is that your brother lightin' a shuck? We'll get him," said the Sheriff. The Sheriff quickly disarmed his prisoner taking a pistol and gun belt, then turned him around, tying his hands with rawhide strips.

Buck Carroll stepped forward to take control of the prisoner. "I found the young one. He's shot up pretty bad. Got him tethered to a tree."

"Where's the Kid?" asked the Sheriff. "I lost track of him when we were pinned down by rifle fire."

Believing that it was Ronnie who had made a get-away, the Sheriff cautiously crossed the roadway to the other side, Colt extended if Ronnie was up to some trick. When the Sheriff came up behind the large boulder that had been used for cover, he found Ronnie laying on the ground, his face bloodied from a large gash on the side of his head. The third bank robber was just beginning to stir.

"Who just rode out of here?" The Sheriff recognized Ronnie by his familial appearance. You got another partner?"

Ronnie groaned and touched his head, his fingers coming back all bloodied. He shook his head slowly. "Damn sumbitch! The Laredo Kid, wearing a badge, just made off with the gold."

"What? The Kid was back here?"

"Got the jump on me. He hit me on the head and made off with the gold."

The Sheriff quickly removed the gun belt and pistol from Ronnie's waist and tied his hands. He led the groggy outlaw back across the roadway toward Buck and the other prisoners. He pushed Ronnie to the ground next to his brothers and swung into the saddle, calling to Buck over his shoulder. "Watch these desperados. I'm going after the other one who just rode away with the gold."

"What? There's another one?" Buck's surprise was obvious.

Chapter 27

The Kid's mind was racing... looking to protect his new treasure.

The tracks from the Kid's horse were clear, deep from the extra weight of the gold, and showing a hard gallop as the Kid pushed his horse to get away. The Sheriff gave a shake of the reins and click of the tongue and a nudge with his boots, and the roan was off and running. In the distance ahead, topping a ridge, he saw the Kid and his horse. Already, the animal looked to be laboring. The roan would close the gap in a hurry.

The Sheriff wondered how much gold had been stolen, and how much it weighed. It was clear that it was a heavy load. The Kid's horse could be carrying an extra fifty or hundred pounds or more of weight. And at a gallop, the weight of the coins will bounce, putting an extra burden on the fleeing animal. The Kid's animal would tire quickly.

The southward trail headed towards the border town of Laredo, the Kid's hometown. He would know the area, its creeks and hollows, and caves. The Sheriff knew he must catch this gunslinger who now was really showing his true colors. He wondered why Smith would have hired this man, a known gunslinger with a hooligan reputation. Buck had said that the man was hired to guard the gold, and no doubt Smith had provided good pay. Yet, given the opportunity to catch the bank robber and return the gold, the Laredo Kid had chosen to take the money from the robber and run.

From a hill, the Sheriff looked down into a hollow created by a meandering creek. The hollow looked to be a mile wide, clear evidence that in rainy periods, a large volume of water had flowed downstream until it merged with Rio Bravo. Along the wandering creek, there was a line of cottonwoods, providing refuge for an animal or person seeking cover and escape from pursuit. A dark spec moved about midway between the Sheriff's position and the cover of the trees and creek. The Speck moved slower now. The Kid's animal had tired and would soon need rest and water.

"We need to catch them before they find cover," said the Sheriff. The roan's ears twitched in acknowledgment. With a click and a nudge, the pursuit was on again.

As he rode into a wide hollow with a creek down below, the Laredo Kid's mind flashed back to this life-changing decision. There was the gold in two canvas bags at Ronnie López's feet. And that idiot López thought he was such a big shot, hiding behind a boulder when that Sheriff was closing fast. The Kid had never seen so much money. Just take it, he thought. It was an opportunity he just couldn't pass up. The Laredo Kid had been confident that he could make it back to Laredo, and leave a trail across the river into Mexico. Just let them try to find him.

But now a new realization was setting in. His horse had been game and had given a good run for many miles. But the load of the gold coins had taken its toll. It seemed like a hundred and fifty pounds, like riding double. But now, the animal was tiring. Up ahead he saw a tree line along a creek. It would be a good place to hide, to rest. He kept urging the tired horse ahead, he had to get there and hide his trail. Maybe the Sheriff would keep on going.

He pushed the animal through the ford and midway, tugged the reins to turn upstream. Once in the water, the horse stopped to drink. The Kid pulled hard on the reins and kicked the horse's ribs to urge him forward. He wanted to get away from the roadway and find a secluded spot to rest, if even for a little bit. He felt a sting on his neck, like some pesky bee angry because of an intruder poking a stick in the hive in search of honey. In the distance, there was a pop, that he realized was gunfire. That sheriff was closer than he realized. He jerked the reins and kicked hard on the horse's ribs to get movement upstream.

The Kid's mind was now racing, looking for a way out, looking for a way to protect his new treasure, the hundred fifty pounds of gold coins. He could sneak through the tree line and make a break farther upstream. But his horse was already weak and tired. Should he bury the coins? Some of it, or all, and sneak away so he could come back later and retrieve it? But he couldn't bear to think of leaving the coins on the chance that the Sheriff or someone else would find the riches.

It was a low spot and the ground was soft here, muddy and marsh-like, thick with bulrush and pondweed. The horse struggled through the muck making noise with splashing hooves in the water and breaking twigs from sapling cottonwood trees. The horse snorted its disagreement and it was all the Kid could do to urge the animal on to put distance between himself and his pursuer.

"Think. Think. There has to be another way." The Laredo Kid's thoughts came out loud now. "Or, I could hide in the dense underbrush and reeds along the creek. But what about the horse? That Sheriff would find the horse and keep looking until he found me. Maybe I could bushwhack the sheriff, take his animal, and then make a break for the border."

Chapter 28

The Sheriff was in awe, watching a dead man walking.

"There'll be no bushwhacking today, Kid. You're in my sights now." Sheriff Holland had the Kid sighted down the barrel of his Winchester. "You're right about one thing, though, I kept looking and I found you. Give it up. Here. Now."

Through the thick greenery of trees and marsh and grasses, a glint of sunlight broke through. From the direction of the voice, a shadow showed the profile of the Sheriff behind the Winchester not more than thirty feet away. Both men were on their horses. In between them lay a marshy mix of tall grass, cottonwood saplings, and several larger trees. The sun was behind the Sheriff's back, making him a shadow while the Kid squinted into the glare with the sun in his face.

The Kid had a smile on his face. This wasn't the first time another gunman had the drop on him and using his wiles, the Kid had lived to face this situation today. "I was hired by Smith to protect his gold. I'm just doing my job, bringing it back to Smith."

"Mighta been a good story if I hadn't had to chase you south towards Laredo," countered the Sheriff.

"My horse took off in the wrong direction and—"

"It don't take ten miles to turn a horse around. Besides, I've got a prisoner named Ronnie López with a gash on his face who says you stole the cash. Put your hands in the air and come on out of that swamp."

The Kid had turned slightly, giving him a better angle to draw. "Maybe we can make a deal. They pay you what? Fifty a month? There's more here-"

"Don't try it—"

The Kid drew and aimed at the shadow, ducking his head behind the horse's neck. He kicked his horse to make it jump. The Sheriff squeezed the trigger without waiting. Two shots banged as one.

The Sheriff's shot hit the gun in the Kid's hand singeing his fingers and causing a cracking sound with a flash of pain in his wrist as the gun flew back and splashed into backwater. The Kid looked down. His right hand felt limp. There was no blood, but the hand now felt numb and useless. His startled horse had splashed in the mud but was unable to get forward movement.

"That som-bitch. I'll get him," growled the Kid glaring at the Sheriff. He pulled his second Colt from the left holster and had it up at the ready with the hand that still worked. Seething, he slid from the saddle into the wet mush and high-stepped splashing forward left arm and Colt extended.

Click-click-BAM. The Sheriff fired again. The Kid jerked; his step hesitated. His Colt spit fire and the Kid stepped forward again haltingly.

The Sheriff watched as the Laredo Kid now staggered his way following a smoking Colt, death in his eyes, a red blotch now growing just above a shiny brass belt buckle. The Kid kept coming, step by stumbling step, like a charging bull in slow motion. The Sheriff was momentarily in awe watching a dead man walking. He had seen this before in other gunfights. The Kid kept coming. Another shot from the Kid's Colt missed but threw splinters from a nearby tree into the Sheriff's face. The Sheriff cocked the rifle again and squeezed the trigger, but the hammer only made a metallic click on the empty chamber.

The Kid had closed to about twenty feet away, now on dry land weaving from a stiff-legged walk, the Colt swinging with each step, the red blotch now filled the front of his shirt and pants. The Sheriff heard the click as the Kid cocked the Colt again and behind it saw the shiny white teeth from the Kid's hard hateful smile.

A seasoned lawman and former Ranger, veteran of many a gunfight, the Sheriff held his ground. He instinctively dropped the rifle and pulled his Colt, cocked, and fired. The first shot tinged into the brass badge pinned to the Kid's shirt causing a gasp as its force knocked the wind out of the gunslinger. The second shot found its mark in the Kid's throat causing blood to spurt to the ground while a dribble of red formed at his lips.

The Kid's face registered surprise and his eyes rose to meet those of the man who had shot him. The Kid's lips quivered as if in an attempt to speak. Then his eyes rolled up and back, and his legs wilted, causing him to drop to his knees and fall face-first to the ground.

Chapter 29

The return trip with two wounded prisoners was slow going.

Ronnie López was suddenly aware of movement. His eyes opened to reveal a man with a sun wrinkled face kneeling over him. He saw a brass badge and recognized the man he and his brothers had been trying to kill. He had a terrible headache and his face was bloody. It was the Sheriff who had been chasing them, chasing them since the bank robbery in the little town on the Texas plains. Across the way, he could see brother Tommie, standing here, forlorn, shackled, looking in his direction.

The Sheriff had returned with the Kid's body and the gold. He and Buck Carroll now had three prisoners, one with bullet wounds as well as two dead deputies to bury. Buck acknowledged that the two new ranch hands had been hired for their gun skills relating to protecting the gold shipment and then catching the robbers. Both were considered to be drifters and not known to have any family. The decision was to bury the gunmen and return to Bent Creek with the gold and valuables and the prisoners. Since Ronnie was still groggy and Tommie was healthy, Tommie's assignment was to dig the graves and bury the two dead deputies under the supervision of deputy Buck Carroll. The Sheriff tended to Bebe López's wounds to prepare him for travel. The remaining sunlight allowed an hour's ride before finding a creek and suitable campsite.

The return trip with two wounded prisoners was a slow-going walking pace. They encountered a rancher and negotiated a deal for use of his supply wagon to haul the injured robbers and put Tommie as the driver knowing that he could not escape using the wagon. Tommie promised not to try to escape, saying that he wanted to make sure that his brother received medical care. Bebe's horse was tethered to the back of the wagon. This arrangement provided an opportunity for the Sheriff and Buck to take up the rear and ride side by side, and talk.

"Riding posse like this must be a nice change of pace from daily chores at the ranch," suggested the Sheriff.

"Work will always be there when I get back," replied Buck.

They rode in silence for another mile. The Smith Ranch foreman was a man of few words. In the years that the Sheriff had known Buck, he had been the ramrod for Smith's ranch, in the background, quiet and efficient. When he spoke, it was of cattle, their care and handling, and giving directions to ranch hands to carry out the chores for managing the herd. Buck was a man to be respected for his skills on a horse and the use of a rope and branding iron, the tools of the cowboy. Buck was also to be respected for his loyalty to the brand. The Sheriff hoped to get Buck to open up a bit on the ride back to town.

"That's a heavy load," said the Sheriff as he glanced down at the three canvas bags tied to the saddle like a saddlebag. It was like carrying a double load. "How's your animal holding up?"

"At this pace, we'll be just fine." The horse was breathing heavily and beginning to sweat.

"Maybe the wagon? Take a load off."

"No way in hell! I'm charged with bringing the gold back." Buck bristled at the thought. "That bunch already killed two good men. Wouldn't want to tempt them again."

The Sheriff nodded in agreement. "Let me know if your animal needs a break. We don't want him to go lame."

Buck acknowledged with a nod. After another mile, the Sheriff pressed again for more. "The gold, is that payroll? Or does James have another deal in the works?"

Buck's eyes bored into the Sheriff in a hard glare as he decided whether to reply. The Sheriff met the glare stone-faced, waiting. The wagon creaked and chains rattled. Hooves thumped the ground occasionally clicking on a small stone. From somewhere nearby, the rich fluty whistle of a meadowlark trilled and was answered by another farther away.

Buck's eyes darted across the horizon, before speaking under his breath. "Boss didn't want to keep too much at the ranch, people talk, you know. Cattle drive funds were kept in the bank in San Antone. But, with the new bank in town, he wanted to have some handy."

The horses thumped along and the wagon jostled on a bump in the two-track. There was a movement to the side as a red-tailed hawk swooped down after a meal, but came up with empty talons.

"Payroll? Likely. 'Nother deal? I ramrod the herd. Boss might share a glass of whiskey at the end of a long day, but he don't share those details with me."

Chapter 30

"I've got a man outside who needs to make a sizeable bank deposit."

The shadows angled across the street as the riders and wagon rolled into town at the end of a long day on the trail. Laughter and the clink of glasses carried to the street from the Cattleman's saloon. Bebe was delivered to Doc's and the other two López brothers were locked into the new cage at the recently re-built sheriff's office. The Sheriff left the roan with hostler Washington at the stable.

Since the bank was closed for the night, the Sheriff checked the saloons for banker Harlan Hawkins. He found Hawkins in the Red-eye along with James Smith. Proprietor Betsy Brown had joined her two prominent customers and the conversation sounded spirited and lively.

"Don't mean to interrupt this little party," said the Sheriff as he approached the table. "But I've got a man outside who needs to make a sizeable bank deposit."

James was on his feet. "You get 'em? Get the gold? Is it all there?"

"At the cost of two lives," said the Sheriff.

"What? Is Buck ok?"

"Outside with three canvas bags and a tired horse."

"Harlan, get off your butt and open your safe," barked James.

James Smith and the banker were already rushing from the room looking for Buck outside. All the patrons had stopped to watch the Sheriff's entrance and the Red-eye servers and staff had gathered by the kitchen door.

"Howdy Miss Betsy. You're looking mighty fine this evening," said the Sheriff as he turned his attention to his dear friend.

"Why, thank you, Clay. I feel like such a mess with these bandages and all." Betsy's smile turned serious. "I'm so glad you made it home safely. Who? You said two lives,…Who?"

"Two men from the Smith Ranch—"

"Who? I know a lot of those boys. They come in from time to time." Betsy's face was etched in concern.

"New hires, not his regular crew. These fellers were,…uh hired guns, not regular ranch hands." By now, the Sheriff was sitting, tired after many long days on the trail.

"Who? I want to know it all."

"Betsy, dear, a man gets a powerful thirst after days on the trail. For the price of a Texas Tickler and dinner, I can tell you the outcome of our little venture." He leaned back and his eyes traced Betsy's lovely form noting an errant wisp of her blond hair dangling close to her left eye. He reached over and with his finger, moved the golden thread behind her ear. "It's really nice to see you out and about. "

With a wave of her hand, Betsy's servers were quick to bring a bottle of the Sheriff's favorite whiskey. And a couple of minutes later a sizzling steak and steaming bowl stew were set before the tired lawman.

"Tell me everything, Clay."

After a few swallows of whiskey to relax and a few juicy bites, the Sheriff began to mellow. He never shared the dirty details of a lawman's life with the fairer sex, with but one exception. His mind flashed back momentarily to the lovely Sarah, and their long talks which sometimes drifted into her queries about his work and the dangers he faced. Now, once again, he sat across from a lovely lady whose demonstrated self-confidence displayed her earnest desire to hear the life and death details that the frontier lawman shared only with his peers. He glanced around the room, to be assured of their privacy, to avoid disclosing gruesome details to others.

"First of all, we got the man who shot you. Then, well, you know Buck. He's, a cowboy's cowboy. Knows cattle, knows his stuff, loyal to Smith, rides for the brand. He brought two new hands, Laredo Kid, and Curt Cousins. But these two weren't ordinary ranch hands. These fellers were gun hands. I knew I'd have my hands full keeping the lid on these two as deputies." The Sheriff told the story of trailing the López brothers, the ride southward, the confrontation with the hotheaded Laredo Kid, the bushwhack ambush that killed Cousins, the renegade theft of the gold by the Kid, his pursuit of the Kid, and the gunplay by the Kid that resulted in his death. They recovered the gold and brought the López's back for justice. The Smith gun-hands lived by the gun, died by the gun, and now lay under the south Texas soil.

Betsy had listened and nodded, absorbing every detail, her reactions varying from eager interest to surprise to sadness in the ultimate deaths of the two Smith hands. In the end, she reached out and held the Sheriff's hand, as her moist eyes released a single tear, saying, "I was so worried. I'm glad you are home safe."

The emotion of tears can be catching. Clay Holland felt his eyes moisten as this beautiful woman touched his hand in reaction to the story. It was like they were the only two people in the world at the moment. There may have been people and activity and noise in the Red-eye, but at this moment in time, the thoughts and feelings and emotions of two became one. With the telling of the story of danger and death and survival, Clay now felt a relief with the release of those gruesome details that normally his mind would sort out in images and dreams that often kept him awake at night. It was those images and dreams that had led to the whiskey for solace and sleep.

Clay thought about the fleetingness of life, the brief period of happiness with his marriage to Sarah, and especially the tough nature of a lawman's justice where longevity was measured by one's wits to avoid danger, but when necessary by skill with a gun. The relief he felt now brought a flashback to Sarah, and with it a feeling of contentment that he had not felt since Sarah's passing. From somewhere deep within, he knew he had Sarah's consent. He got down on one knee.

"Miss Betsy Brown, will you be my wife?"

##

About the Author

About the author: William S. Hubbartt is the author of fiction and non-fiction books. His western fiction work includes Six Bullet Justice, Justice for Abraham, and Blazing Guns on the Santa Fe Trail. He is the author of the new novel Drawing a Line: A look inside the corporate response to sexual harassment and several management books including Achieving Performance Results – Boosting performance in the virtual workplace. Hubbartt's short stories have appeared in anthologies, literary journals, and E-zines.

Author's note: English-Spanish translations appearing in this story used Google translator and Microsoft translator.

Books by William S. Hubbartt

Western Fiction
Clint Carrigan Adventures
Against Overwhelming Odds 2022
Live and Die by the Gun 2021
Blazing Guns on the Santa Fe Trail 2020
Clay Holland Adventures
Lawman's Justice 2020 * (Saga #3 and Saga #4)
Justice for Abraham 2020* (Saga #2)
Six Bullet Justice 2020* (Saga #1)
*First appeared as E-books under Outlaws Publishing label
Contemporary Fiction
Drawing a Line: A look inside the corporate response to sexual harassment 2020
Melton's Mettle (Coming soon)

Non-fiction
Achieving Performance Results: Boosting Performance in the Virtual Workplace 2019
HIPPA Privacy Sourcebook 2004
The HIPPA Security Rule 2004
The Medical Privacy Rule 2002
The New Battle Over Workplace Privacy 1998
Personnel Policy Handbook: How do develop a manual that works 1993
Performance Appraisal Manual for Managers and Supervisors 1992

Reader comments on Hubbartt's western tales*
Well written with plenty of actions and a sweet ending! J.
A good western historical story. C.
It's a fast & smooth easy read. M.
…fraught with peril, and mostly exciting. G.
This is an excellent read for the genre. D.
A good western in an unusual milieu for the genre. G.
Another excellent story in this 1870's Wild West Series. S.

* From reader reviews in Amazon books and Goodreads

Made in the USA
Las Vegas, NV
28 July 2023

75334924R00118